I0630727

BEYOND
LOVECRAFT

FRANK FORTE

BEYOND LOVECRAFT

Published by Asylum Press

Office of Publication:

Asylum Press

P.O. Box 4281

Glendale, CA 91202 USA

Email: mailto:AsylumPressComics@gmail.com

http://www.asylumpress.com

Cover Illustration Copyright © 2020 by Frank Forte

Cover design by Frank Forte

Editing by Michael Du Plessis and Elizabeth J. Musgrave

BEYOND LOVECRAFT

© 2020 Frank Forte

All rights reserved.

TABLE OF CONTENTS

FOREWARD

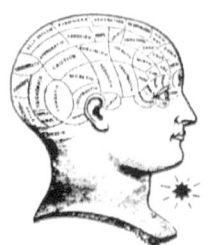

Welcome to Lovecraft World, or, It's H.P. Lovecraft's Cosmos and We Just Live in It

"That is not dead which can eternal lie; And with strange aeons even death may die," so wrote Abdul Alhazared, the compiler of the *Necronomicon*, that fatal compendium of lore about the Older Gods—especially the terrifying bewinged deity with a faceful of tentacles who sleeps (for the time being) under the sea. Indeed, for proof that immortality can follow dormancy, we need only follow the posthumous life of Howard Philips Lovecraft, from whose febrile imaginings, Alhazred, the *Necronomicon* and Cthulhu all spring. Lovecraft is perhaps one of the most extraordinary of American writers, whose works have a taloned hold on our world that very few other writers have managed—hyperbole earned by Lovecraft's incalculable impact on contemporary popular culture.

As recognizable as Poe's Raven, the Misfits skull and Mickey Mouse ears, Cthulhu tentacles undulate everywhere in 2020.

Thus, a search for Cthulhu on Amazon gets me T-shirts, one for "Great Old Ones Grog" (it's "a funny Lovecraft [sic] spoof," the product description adds), one with the presidential slogan *Cthulhu 2020*, another with an image of a key pad to accept or decline the (cellphone) call of Cthulhu. There are Cthulhu rainbow polyhedral dice (for *Dungeons and Dragons*), a be-tentacled resin drinking goblet, a plastic Cthulhu outline as parody of the fish bumper ornament, a Cthulhu clock, videos, one called "Call Girl of Cthulhu," another about Cthulhu and climate change, a Cthulhu lapel pin, and, perhaps most appealingly, a glow-in-the dark "C Is for Cthulhu" plush toy.

Even a search for "Lovecraft" gets me the new HBO TV series, *Lovecraft Country*, the novel on which it's based and a comedy, *The Last Lovecraft* (indeed), before any actual books by H.P. Lovecraft.

Yet for all this, Lovecraft is a writer, a maker of worlds through words, and it is in and through writing, that Lovecraft's works comes most alive. Going beyond Lovecraft, in the title of this anthology, that you, dear reader, are perusing, means going back to him, as here, in the fevered—and wily--creations of Frank Forte.

When Howard Philips Lovecraft died in 1937 at the age of 47 in the near-poverty that he had experienced most of his life, he was a writer whose success had been limited primarily to the pulp magazine, *Weird Tales*. He had built a circle of writer-friends—Clark Ashton Smith, Robert Howard (creator of *Conan the Barbarian*), August Derleth, Donald Wandrei, Frank Belknap Long, Robert Bloch (the creator of Psycho)—all of who are worth reading in their own right. His wide and witty correspondence with them provided an escape from his otherwise miserable life.

Lovecraft's work, republished by the small press Arkham

House in somewhat limited runs, then rereleased in paperback form in the 1970s remained the providence of a cult audience, unafraid of Lovecraft's style—unashamedly anachronistic with a delight in arcane words such as "tarn" and "batrachian."

A scholar of Gothic, fantasy and horror literature—the author of a monograph called *Supernatural Horror in Fiction* (1927, revised through 1934)--Lovecraft was keenly aware of his place in a canon that included Edgar Allen Poe as well as lesser-known writers such as Lord Dunsany, Algernon Blackwood, Robert Chambers, and Arthur Machen.

In both his impact and his fondness for older traditions of literature, Lovecraft resembles his British contemporary J.R.R. Tolkien. If the rather genteel Tolkien wrote a ponderous epic, Lovecraft worked, by comparison, in miniature. Very few of his texts approach novel length (*At the Mountains of Madness* is one exception). Like his idol, Poe, Lovecraft worked almost exclusively in short fiction. While the brevity may have been shaped by the demands of magazine publishing, Lovecraft's imaginative expansiveness astonishes. *The Lord of the Rings* insists in its length on its own importance, but Lovecraft's short fictions burst far beyond anything like the world creation of Middle Earth. His imagination refuses boundaries, fearing yet reveling in the enormity of space and the vastness of time. He creates in the Cthulhu mythos a modern mythic cycle of the Old Gods—beings malign and divine who far predate anything resembling humanity and even anything resembling earth. After all, Lovecraft is the inventor of the genre called "cosmic horror."

For all his apparent fustiness, pastiches of Romantic and Edwardian texts, and his modeling of both himself and his prose on 18th-century models, Lovecraft is essentially modern—his cosmos is the one of deep time and limitless space.

With such enormous ambitions, it seems to be a benevolent poetic justice that Lovecraft's creations have moved out of a small circle of fans and presses to engulf, if not perhaps the entire universe itself, at least the universe of culture. In terms of the quality of his writing, Lovecraft's works have been considerably reassessed—while the influential high culture critic Edmund Wilson remarked sourly on Lovecraft's "bad art" and "bad taste" in the 1950s, contemporary cultural commentators as different as Veronica Nelson and Michel Houellebecq insist on the value of Lovecraft's art, the incantatory delights of his language, the irresistible rhythms of his prose. Lovecraft's verbal charms—his "Lovecraftese"--have gained a permanent place in a contemporary lexicon. How else would we all know the word "eldritch"?

But if Lovecraft is everywhere right now, Frank Forte's collection *Beyond Lovecraft* takes us both beyond Lovecraft and back to Lovecraft—it's a grim, ghastly, horrid, gruesome, and, yes, eldritch re-imagining, rewriting and re-invention that is simultaneously a return to Lovecraft.

In this collection the old and the new, sphinxes and bioengineering, woodland walks and autopsies, the familiar and the utterly strange come together. In Forte's stories, as in Lovecraft's, concision drives the point home. For everyone who can never have enough Lovecraft, this present collection of Forte's works inspired by H.P.L., begins with the reassuring only to unsettle us.

As all good horror should do.
Welcome.
Dare to step inside--and to step beyond.
Michael Du Plessis

Richmond, VA, September 2020

INTRODUCTION

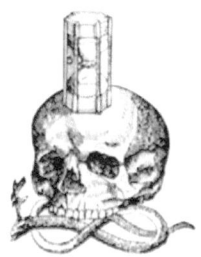

"The one test of the really weird is simply this—whether or not there be excited in the reader a profound sense of dread, and of contact with unknown spheres and powers; a subtle attitude of awed listening, as if for the beating of black wings or the scratching of outside shapes and entities on the known universe's utmost rim. "~ Howard Phillips Lovecraft "Supernatural Horror in Literature" November 1925 to May 1927

Growing up an adolescent in the 80s, I was exposed to the video store and all of its wonders on VHS. The horror boom of the 1980s brought many a terror and gore filled flick that sported an illustrated cover. As a youth who loved all things scary, these movies were hard to resist.

I can't remember if I had seen Stuart Gordon and Brian Yuzna's *Re-Animator* and *From Beyond* before I had read the pages of the H.P. Lovecraft collections Random House had released. These tomes displayed amazing and terrifying covers by artist Michael Whelen and these were the books that I would spend my nights getting acquainted with this Master of Horror Literature.

With descriptions for *The Tomb and Other Tales* such as: *"This extraordinary collection features 13 spine-tingling tales of delicious terror by the unquestioned master of the horror genre, as well as portions of stories he never fully completed"* How could I not be enthralled?

There were other Lovecraftian adaptations to be found in comics, graphic novels, and images by numerous artists and illustrators. Chasoium's *Call of Cthulhu* role playing game soon hit the market and I could now live the world of Randolph Carter and Charles Dexter Ward instead of just reading about them on the pages.

I soon discovered the works of August Derleth and Clark Ashton Smith inspired by HPL that were published under the Arkham House imprint. Other authors like Robert E. Howard and Robert Bloch had also penned tales inspired by Lovecraft and even used his mythos and locations for many of their tales. I realized there were probably too many Lovecraftian inspired stories for me to read in a lifetime.

Not long after discovering all of these authors who were influenced by Lovecraft, I decided to write my own stories. At nineteen, I collaborated with Mike Bliss. Al Columbia and Scott DiAngelis to create the comic book horror anthology *From Beyonde*, a nod to the master himself. The book lasted four issues and included short experimental comic stories that were loosely inspired by HPL, David Lynch, Vaughn Oliver, The Pixies, Berni Wrightson, Graham Ingels, Stuart Gordon, John Carpenter, Bill Sienkiewicz and many others.

Upon reading HPL's works, I also stumbled upon his letters where it was revealed he was a racist and held white supremacist beliefs. This was troubling to me, as a fan and it would be to anyone who read Lovecraft and thought his works were incredible and inspiring. I grappled with how to separate the artist and his creations from the man himself.

Truth be told, H.P. Lovecraft's trademark fantastical creatures and supernatural thrills have influenced some of today's important writers and filmmakers, including Stephen King, Alan Moore, F. Paul Wilson, Guillermo del Toro, and Neil Gaiman. I'm sure these masters have all struggled with HPL the writer and his appalling beliefs. Regardless of Lovecraft's views, his fiction has been read by fans for over a century now, and I'm sure it will go on for another hundred years.

Recently, I had the honors of working as a storyboard artist on HBO's *Lovecraft Country*, based on the novel by Matt Ruff. The show has earned critical acclaim from critics and fans across the globe. The show's juxtaposition of Jim Crow-era racism and otherworldly terror chronicles the story of Atticus (Tic) Freeman and his family and friends as they travel across the country in search of Tic's roots. What they find is more unfathomable than they could have ever imagined.

H.P. Lovecraft continues to inspire a new generation of storytellers. I can only imagine what the next incarnation of horrors will be.

Frank Forte

Los Angeles,

September 2020

JOIN MY NEWSLETTER

I try to publish new books often. I also create comics and fine art when I'm not creating storyboards for shows like Lovecraft Country, Solar Opposites and Bob's Burgers. I wake up, drink coffee, write stories, draw, watch TV, exercise, sleep, then repeat.

If you'd like to be notified when a new book, comic or art show is about to happen sign up below and I'll give you a quick heads up with direct links when that happens. I also appear regularly at conventions like Comic-Con and Wondercon and I'll announce those dates as well. Nothing more nothing less.

JOIN MY NEWSLETTER

ASPHINXIATION

The annex for Occult Studies of Miskatonic University was located at the north end of the campus. I had a small office, but I had decorated it with artifacts and memorabilia from my various adventures. My most recent excursion to Egypt was a delve into some mysterious findings surrounding The Sphinx, that had enriched me with an ebon statue which was prominently displayed on my desk.

"Dr. Darius, may we come in?" a voice came from outside my door.

"Dr. Olivea, Dr. Rodia' thank god you're here, " I couldn't hold back my enthusiasm to relate my findings to my most trusted peers and academic colleagues.

"The notes on my latest archeological discovery are almost completed, " I could barely get the words out.

"Ah, yes, Dr. Darius, your notes on the impending doom for

all of humanity," Dr. Olivea stated with what seemed like was a whisper of sarcasm.

"Impending doom?" Dr. Rodia said with a lifted eyebrow.

"Yes, Dr. Rodia. Dr. Darius has made a startling discovery inside the sphinx, "Dr. Olivea revealed. I didn't like his tone.

"In the sphinx?" Dr. Rodia replied with a scant tone of ridicule.

"Quite fascinating, isn't it?" Dr. Olivea continued his scoffing. But just under his breath as I could tell, as skeptical as they were, they were eager to hear of my discoveries.

"Tell Dr. Rodia the story you told me, Dr. Darius, " Dr. Rodia egged me on. "Enlighten him on the coming of the *end of all that is.*"

I began my disturbing tale fro the beginning.

It all started three years ago. I was awarded a grant from the national geographic society to begin a new series of excavations in the Valley of the Kings. At first, we found a large collection of artifacts in a newly discovered series of tombs. On the walls were the typical hieroglyphics; nothing was out of the ordinary. Soon our digs were coming up empty, and my grant money was running out. I pleaded for more funds, I tried to tell them if I could just keep going a little longer I'd be sure to find something incredible. But the shortsighted fools in charge of the coffers decided to fund a study to see if rats can understand the Japanese language when spoken backwards. I was livid! Those idiots have no idea of the possibilities of ancient Egypt.

Me, Dr. Darius, the greatest archeologist in the entire world!"

"Bah," I thought. I wished a pox on them and their

politically correct ignorance!'"

I sought solace from my woes in a bottle of Cheap gin at a local Watering hole.

There an old man approached me. He was mumbling some Arabic gibberish and Begging for alms."

I gave him the last of my copper coins. In return, much to my Surprise he gave me a large leather bound Book. I thought nothing of it, but that night, as I sat alone in my Tent, I examined the ancient book. I noticed it had arcane markings on the inside. They were foreign and strange, but not totally unknown to me, a self-appointed expert in the field of the occult.

It soon occurred to me it was an original copy of the famed and feared Necronomicon...the book of the dead. The bible to the Occult!

As I translated the Arabic text, I was filled with both wonder and Horror. The book Spoke of a time when the earth was inhabited by a race of gods...or perhaps the correct term was.... a race of demons!

The next day I consulted a local occultist about the authenticity of the book I had received. The man burst into a fit of rage and began to warn me about the dangers of the book I now possessed. He insisted I get rid of it at once and that I never gaze upon its accursed pages again. He told me never to return. Knowing for sure that my mysterious tome was indeed authentic impelled me to study it further. Astonishing was the relationship between the drawings in the Necronomicon and the ancient Egyptian monoliths and statues.

Some of the writings, however, were so alien they matched no known alphabet, hieroglyphics or occult writing anywhere in the world.

The book repeatedly mentioned a race of ancient and powerful gods who now lay dormant beneath the earth.

It was this race that built the great sphinx! The oldest and most mysterious structure in all of Egypt!

But more intriguing was the mention of a doorway between the two front legs of the sphinx. As a graduate student I had personally examined the sphinx and knew no doorway existed."

X-ray tests have proven the sphinx to be solid with no voids or cavities of any excessive volume. Naturally, I was skeptical.

That night, with the book and my flashlight, I proceeded from the camp, by the cover of darkness to stand before the Great Sphinx.

Following the instructions in the ancient tome, I read the passage of opening while making the hand gestures described.

I felt like a fool! I'm a scientist, I thought, not an empty headed occultist! Yet, before me, in my disbelief... a doorway appeared. I was in a state of shock, yet I was ever the scientist and I had to examine what was/surely the find of the century. The corridor before me was long and narrow. The bas-reliefs on the sandstone walls depicted animals and creatures that had long since been extinct. Some of the picto-glyphs were so alien to me that I didn't know if they were the fanciful imagination of the artist or if they were a type unknown to science. Soon I realized I had seen these images before...it was in the pages of the Necronomicon!

There was an obvious Connection between the Centuries old book of Black magic and this Secret and ancient Cavern. The corridor went on for what seemed like miles, the mind shattering hieroglyphs were disrupting my perceptions of reality. Perhaps it was only a few hundred yards, but it seemed like I had been Walking for an eternity.

When I finally reached the end of the corridor there stood a giant stone doorway. Its macabre hieroglyphs beckoned me ever closer. I was mesmerized by the ancient gold encrusted carving that was placed in the center of the tri-sectioned door. It was *The Cthulhu-Stone!* Just as described in the *Necronomicon*. It took some time, but deciphered and recited the proper incantations

I easily broke the seal. Was a vast chamber of untold riches behind it? Was it an ancient tomb of gods? Or demons!? Those fools at the national geographic society didn't have the intestinal fortitude to go the distance with me and my genius! So this find was mine! All mine!!

I opened the door.

I stood in awe at the sight before me. It was a vast subterranean city! It was an awesome architectural megalopolis...but pulsing with evil! I could feel it. Each edifice seemed to breathe like living metal. I realized that I had discovered the ancient underground city of *Ry'leh!* A creation that is definitely not of this world! Aeons old or not, the city was breathing...it was alive!

This was not a burial chamber, but a prison...a prison of demons! Unnamable demons! They were awakening after countless millennia of exile...and it was I who had released them! Then I witnessed a sight not meant for human eyes. The demons were slowly emerging from their aeons old slumber! The sound of their soul-shattering screams, as they echoed throughout the vast chamber, will be forever grafted to me soul. It was as if I had thrown open the very gates of hell!! The glyphs on the corridor were a warning! A warning of an unstoppable oblivion that awaits the world should one so foolish to break the seal of the old ones, the great and evil race of alien gods that have lain dormant for centuries. Since ancient times the sphinx has been a symbol of good, its presence said to ward off evil, the perfect guard dog to a prison of demons. How could I have been such a fool?! It was me who unleashed the *Hordes of Hades!!*

The dreaded CTHULHI and YOG-SOTHOTH WOULD SOON BEGIN THEIR REIGN OF TERROR UPON THE EARTH. I fled down the corridor with the hungry cries of the demons from beyond creation close behind me. When I exited the Sphinx I quickly sealed the secret doorway! I knew this was only buying time for the earth...time to gather our forces to meet the onslaught of angry demonic armies as they will surely find a way through the ancient rock that entombs them. My mind reeling in terror and shame, I fled the sphinx. Stumbling across the desert, I collapsed in the sand. A few hours later, luckily, I was found.

"...and brought back here! So now I'm writing my thesis to present to the United Nations. I must write everything down and be sure not to forget any details. THE EARTH MUST BE WARNED!" I shouted at my colleagues Dr. Olivea and Dr. Rodia. I was a ranting lunatic. I knew it. I tried to compose myself.

"Here, Dr. Olivea take this," I handed him a stack of paper. They were my notes from the expedition that I hadn't shown anyone.

"It's the first one thousand pages of my final draft! Have them copied for me...IT'S URGENT!"

"NOW, LEAVE ME! I MUST KEEP WRITING!'" I said as I continued my frantic scribbling.

I could hear the fools outside my office.

"Dr. Olivea, I don't understand. All of Dr. Darius' notes are blank," Dr. Rodia said with a strange curiosity.

Ha. The fools can't even decipher the writings of a genius.

"Of course, Dr. Rodia," Dr. Olivea continued, "you see, as their doctor, I do believe it is important for my 'clients' to live out their little fantasies, but you didn't think we'd give them anything sharp to write with now, did you?

"What?" I thought, "What the hell was he talking about?"

I looked around and realized I wasn't in my office at all. I was in what seemed like a padded cell. Started, I looked at my hand and realized I hadn't been writing with a pencil at all. My index finger was a bloody stump. I looked at the scattered pages around me and they were covered in blood. I didn't see the carful writings of a genius archaeologist, but the frenzied chicken scratchings of a madman!

I thought for a moment, had I imagined everything? The chamber in the Sphinx? The Necronomicon? The city of Ry'leh?

No. It was impossible. My mind was sound. It was just those demonic forces getting into my head. They were making me hallucinate. I was not mad! I was as sane as the human eye!

I must keep writing. The world must know of the dangers that are about to descend upon it. I alone, Dr. Darius, will be the one man who stops the dreaded Cthulhu and Yog-Sothoth from devouring humanity.

I alone will make them see the truth!!!

THE HOUSE AT THE END
OF THE STREET

My morbid curiosity had nagged at me for the better part of two decades. For years I had walked by it, too frightened to get too close, too worried about the fabled curses that would defile anyone who went inside it. I had been too superstitious, a monstrosity that had mocked me as a youth had still persisted to make me cringe to this very day. But today, I was going to push my fears aside and traverse the barriers in my mind that had held me back for so long. I was going to enter the *house at the end of the street.*

For years the Victorian edifice had seemed to deride me, playing on my childhood fears and filling my head with nightmares of ghouls and apparitions. Childish superstitions had given way to adult mental disorders and after years of therapy, my psychiatrist assured me that the only way to conquer my fears was to confront them head on.

There it was, sitting for decades, a decrepit wooden mausoleum resembling a crumbling artifact from some forgotten time. A three story Victorian that at one time stood proud and tall, an example of prosperity in this New England town of Winsted, Connecticut.

As a youth I would listen to tales of horror, as the neighborhood children would spin fanciful tales of torture and murder that occurred upon its grounds. Many a late night campfire I would sit with eager eyes and ears, as these tales would infect my mind as an incurable virus would. They would percolate and grow more horrid as I would replay them inside my head again and again.

There was the tale of Mrs. Pines who lived there in 1845 with her husband who met a mysterious and sudden death. It was said she poisoned him with a mixture of arsenic in his coffee and watched him suffer as he choked and suffocated on his own blood. The story was told that after his burial she dug him up and brought the rotting corpse into her basement where she continued to torment him for decades more until her own death in 1872. It was said that both ghosts haunt the place as they chase each other around the house night after night, Mrs. Pines attempting to poison Mr. Pines again, and Mr. Pines trying to exact his revenge.

There was also the tale of young Bobby Robertson who lived there in the early 1900s with his parents and twin sisters. It was said the sisters were insane, but the mother refused to commit them to an asylum. Bobby's mother insisted that Bobby take care of his deranged siblings and as hard as he tried their mental deterioration was irreversible. An unsound mind will only get worse without proper treatment and that's exactly what happened. The sister's psychopathic disease was that of constant verbal and physical torment of poor Bobby. They would constantly threaten his life, stick him with pins and needles and put little sharp metal objects into his soup. As the story goes, Bobby had enough of this, and one night in their sleep, he took a knife to their throats and ended their harassment forever. He then proceeded to take his bloody cutlery to his mother's room where he proceeded to cut and stab her jugular until her face was unrecognizable. Then Bobby turned the knife on himself, as the realization of the horrors he had just committed was too much for him. Legend says that their ghosts haunted the house and anyone coming in contact with them would be tormented and bedeviled for 30 nights. Many could not go on and before the 30th moon the said harassee would end his own life, just to make it stop.

It was rumored that one Eunice Berkhead also resided in the house at the end of the street. A woman in her elder years, Eunice had dealt with mental disease for quite some time. Whether it was schizophrenia or depression or some other ailment of the psyche, she refused treatment of any kind. Finally succumbing to the voices in her head, old Eunice decided to end her life with a noose. So up to the attic she went and wrapped a burly rope around her neck and kicked out the chair from under her, expecting the world to go black. To Eunice's surprise genetics had given her an unusually strong vertebrae and in combination with her frail body, there wasn't enough weight pulling down to choke her out. She dangled there for days, suffering and strangling, attempting to free herself from the doomed predicament. Eventually, the asphyxiation took over and Eunice expired, her corpse rotting for weeks before anyone found her. Rumor has it that anyone venturing up to the attic would be coerced, by the ghost of Eunice herself, into putting that same noose around their neck and dangling 'til death.

My personal favorite was the tale of Dr. Dencourt. Being a fan of mad doctors since I saw the black and white version of

Frankenstein in my youth, this fable was the one I liked to tell over and over again, even embellishing as I went along. The story was that the insane Dr. Dencourt was a local physician who was banned from practice because of numerous malpractice suits and mysterious "deaths" of patients in his care. Autopsies on the victims revealed syringe marks and the presence of an unknown substance in their blood. Unable to prove what this substance was, there was no way to prove the doctor was guilty of murder or manslaughter. Insisting he was trying to save his patients by administering a proven treatment from the Far East, the township decided he was a snake-oil salesman who had taken it a step too far. He was banned from practicing medicine and his credentials were revoked. Instead of leaving town, he set up shop in the house's basement and kept up with his experiments to find a cure-all drug to prove to the town once and for all he had their best interests at heart. Having no one to experiment on but himself, he began injecting his own arm with these mystery cures. Eventually, these injections caused an infection for which there was no cure. Dr. Dencourt died a slow death in his own subterranean laboratory and his apparition still lurks there to this day, waiting to stick any passers-by with his rusty syringe.

Tales of ghosts and ghouls roaming the house and its acreage persisted for the entirety of my youth. None of these stories could ever be substantiated, as multiple trips to the libraries microfiche room never produced any newspaper articles that proved any of these horrid murders had ever occurred. Never the less the fear of this wooden residence pervaded the entire town. Not even the local real estate agents would even list it. No one was ever interested in buying it. And the many house-flippers who took the most derelict homes and turned them over for profit, never even looked in its direction.

Even in high school, when the fairer sex and adult libations became a priority, we needed a place to sneak off to. My friends and I desired a clubhouse to meet or an abandoned locale to consort, but this house was firmly prohibited. No friend or acquaintance of mine would ever set foot on its premises.

As I approached its three-acre parcel, I peered over the overgrown lot with bleakness. What this place could have been without the terrible rumors and stories that persisted for decades. The wooden fence surrounding it had long been rotting away and many a raccoon or coyote had wandered into in environs. No harm came to them ever. Was it their own ignorance of the ghastly tales of terror that made them unafraid? Didn't animals sense evil and foreboding and stay away from its premises? Yet there were birds and rodents all about. This solidified my theory that these centuries old rumors had gotten the better of the town and the generations of abhorrent stories had percolated into a demented mass hysteria.

No, I thought. This house was as haunted as my little pinky finger.

For the moment that thought entered my head, it vacated just as quickly. I looked up upon the Victorian architecture and marveled at its once prominence in New England society. The house seemed to drop in the middle and its many roofs sagged. No longer did it display straight lines and taught angles of a dignified dwelling, it resembled a spectacle of weather-beaten abandon.

The windows had all been shattered from decades of teenage boys perfecting their rock throwing abilities. I, myself, had tossed many a granite projectile into it's many openings, hoping the sound of a crash or splinter would suggest a direct hit on some interior element or forgotten piece of furniture.

The front yard had many overgrown weeds wrapping

themselves around what remained of the stone edifices that had once been an ornamental garden of some kind. Year after year of neglect had caused the layers of dead overgrowth to accumulate into a perennial creature of its own design.

I stood at the front iron gate and took one last deep breath before I crossed the perimeter of what separated me from the nightmares of my youth. Could I really go through with this? I asked myself. Yes. YES! Of course, I could. How could a grown man let the superstitions of youth get the better of him? How could the irrational fears of paranormal ghosts and goblins hold fast in a strong and willful mind? They couldn't! And any last minute doubts I had were vanquished as I pushed forth the iron gate and entered. Long since had the chain and padlock been removed by various teens who had dared each other to enter these so-called haunted grounds. The shackles that prevented one from going forward into this ominous abyss were merely a push against a rusty metal conduit.

I was over the threshold. And after my nerves had calmed, I wondered what the decades of fear was all about. I was in the front yard of an old abandoned house. That was it. No death. No possession. No abominations attacking my ethereal persona. I knew it. All along I had avoided this place for fear of dying on the spot, or for being haunted by malevolent spirit until I took my own life. Ha, I thought, what a joke.

I moved to the front door. A large thick oak portal it was, with an oxidized knocker that hadn't been used in centuries. Should I use it and alert the local apparitions that I was about to infiltrate their humble abode?

The sound of the fossilized metal latch slamming against iron echoed through the house. What seemed like a cruel joke perpetrated by me against these imagined phantasms seemed for an instant like a bad idea. What if I had alerted some demonic wraiths to my presence and they did not take a fancy to it?

The door creaked open as I peered into the cobweb-covered foyer that introduced me to the forbidden house at the end of the street. Dark and musty it was and insects scattered across the floor as I entered. Surely they had not seen any human visitor in centuries. I closed the door then stopped for a second. I decided to jam a piece of wood I found on the floor between the doorframe and door. Would a ghastly apparition slam the door shut and lock me inside? Ha! I chuckled, of course not. But a breeze could do it. Or raccoon or possum, by accident maybe? I thought it would be best to be confident I had an easy way out. I had no idea if the old latches would jam and I'd be stuck inside, only to be late for dinner. My wife indeed would not approve of that.

The living room was, as one would expect from the late 1800s. I'd seen similar furniture in the staging of homes in historical Colonial towns in Virginia that attempted to envisage times of yesteryear. Some of the chairs had been covered by sheets that now took on a morbid brown color and were most certainly not the sterile white they once held. A layer of dust covered all surfaces and my navigating through the room stirred it up in a way that invaded my nasal cavities and throat. I began to sneeze and cough, wondering if there were perhaps some rat feces in the particles. I knew that ingesting rodent fecal matter could be harmful or even fatal. My trusty handkerchief was all I needed to prevent this occurrence, and luckily it was in my jacket pocket. A quick loop and a tie and I was safe from any deadly mists that may come my way.

The house itself held a dark ambiance. The walls were cast in a brown tone; not a cream or eggshell that was popular nowadays. This gave way to darker shadows and what seemed like eerie movements on the walls and window frames. I chuckled. I was not going to give in to my adolescent fears and fanciful imagination. Those were either scared cockroaches or other insects scampering away for fear of me.

As I made my way to the kitchen, a horrific chill came over me as I noticed the cutlery still displayed on a center table that was most likely used to prepare the daily meals. A knife, most likely from the 19th century, was laid out for me to see. Upon closer examination, I could see what looked like a sanguine stain upon its blade. I quickly corrected myself. No, it was over a century of rust and corrosion. Dried blood! My youthful nightmarish creativity was working intensely. The kitchen wasn't where some terrible murder had occurred, it was simply a place where food was prepared and joyous meals were shared with loving groups of family and friends.

My wandering eyes travelled across the floor where I saw piles of broken glass, ceramic plates and other ephemera often find in a cookery. I walked carefully as I didn't want to lacerate my foot and chance an infection by a rusty nail. I had a bad reaction to a tetanus shot a few years ago and the thought of getting another made me extremely cautious where to walk.

I grabbed an old broom from a closet and used that to push around the piles of debris in hopes of uncovering some grisly clue to an even more atrocious crime. To my surprise, under the dust and grime I unveiled a small bottle of what looked like poison. The skull and bones were part of the milky glass that the vessel was comprised of. It was surely not of this era.

Could this have been the bottle of arsenic used my the bloodthirsty Mrs. Pines to do her husband in? Was this the sinister vial that held the toxin that invaded Mr. Pines organs and caused a prolonged and painful demise? What foolishness, I thought, as I corrected myself. These types of visions were to be expected when one mixes an eerie setting with childhood folklore. One tries to rationalize internal fears, and the outcome could be unpredictable.

I was exposing myself to a strange background of enfeebled surroundings behind the ghoulish hints of nightmares and the wild whispers of a creaking old house; one can hardly expect to be wholly free from mental tension.

The stairs to the second floor presented a peculiar problem. They were cracked and exhibited holes that exposed the dark chasm below. I had to navigate to the upstairs in order to fully quell my fears, but how to do that was a problem. I deduced that if I maintained a steady course and kept my weight to the edges of the stairs, where the beams had more stability, I could make my way upward. Slowly, I took step after step and shuddered every time I heard a creak and a crack, which was at just about every time I put a foot forward. Looking down into the menacing blackness that was behind the broken and fractured stairs, I wondered if perhaps a small child was swallowed up whole by these splintered mouths. Was there an infantile carcass lying in between the walls waiting to be put to rest in the ground? Its soul wandering in purgatory waiting for the sacred rights to be performed on its earthly form.

Blast! Again I am whisked away into some bizarre fantasy of death and dread. Visualizing the demise of a young child by a house with a mind of its own. I should be writing down these tales, as I could be a celebrated writer of suspenseful terrors in my own right with yarns such as these.

I soon emerged onto the second floor. I was greeted by a flock of pigeons that had made their home there. I almost stumbled back as the panicked foul swooped past me like a frenzied horde. Gaining my footing, I looked about and noticed the floors were covered in bird droppings and feathers from wall to wall. The stench of mold and decay crept into my nostrils as my thin handkerchief was no barrier from the horrid stench.

The lines and curves of the upstairs hallway were of a deformed nature. Gravity had taken over and the entire house sank on its now contorted frame. I could not gain stability or balance as the floors too were twisted and warped like some Coney Island funhouse. A slight dizziness came over me, and I placed both hands on the peeling walls to steady myself. Were the contorted floorboards to blame or the putrid stench? Perhaps both. I continued on. Coming this far was more than I had anticipated and I was not about to terminate my journey now. The annihilation of my childhood fears was close at hand.

The first room I encountered looked like it had belonged to a young boy at one time. A small bed stood at one side of the room with a wooden desk sized for a grade school child. A small wooden box lie on its side and a few broken and dust covered toys were strewn about. A small iron cast fire engine and what looked like a wild west cowboy were lying as if they'd been entombed in a coffin of dredge.

Could this have been the room of young Bobby Robertson, the boy who was driven crazy by his unhinged twin sisters? Get a grip, I told myself, as this could be the bedroom of any number of boys over the last two centuries. Surely not that of a youthful homicidal maniac.

My next stop was another small bedroom on the other side of the hall. The windows shattered, as were all the windows in the house, and the scattering of many projectiles that were launched from afar, hitting their targets with a disorderly precision that comes with late night vandalism. The room had split floorboards and a double vanity along with a broken double decker bunk bed. The bedroom of Bobby's two sisters? Dorothy and Judith Robertson? It couldn't be. I had convinced myself these fanciful tales of terror were just the product of imaginative youth and fireside fiction.

I moved forward to the large bedroom at the end of the hall. An addled queen-size bed was set at an off angle in the center of the room. Debris and feces were littered about, as this was obviously the lair of some type of vermin. The stench was undeniably rancid as my eyes began to water. Maybe these airborne particulates were invading my lungs and causing distress and a festering affliction that would manifest itself in the coming hours or days. I needn't stay here and conjure up thoughts of Mrs. Pines or any other dozens of homicidal maidens who permeated childhood scary tales.

The sounds of scratching and scurrying could be heard coming from within the house's walls. The atrocious racket chaffed at the insides of my mind, begging me to turn back. I had to resist the temptation to recoil. I had to see this through.

My last stop was the attic, the pinnacle of the origin of my irrational fears and phobias. The place where the crazed elderly woman Eunice Berkhead had attempted to take her own life by hanging, but by some cruel act of fate and a failing rope, she hung there for days and suffered. Thinking about her deed, she wished nothing more than to take it back, only to ultimately succumb to the choking grasp of the twisted twine. Her tormented spirit resided in the garret of the house forever more, tormenting impressionable others to commit the same awful suicidal crime.

I creaked my way up the thin corridor of stairs leading to the drafty loft that was the highest point of the house. I rose slowly as my head peaked into the shadowy tangles of crumbling musty-smelling alcoves and rotting rafters. The foul smelling room was strewn with boxes and forgotten antiques from a bygone age. Ancient bird nests and squirrel dwellings could be seen in every corner of the expanse.

To my shock and astoundment, I peered up at a decayed noose hanging from the ceiling. It could not be! This was exactly what my mind had conjured from the fictitious tales of horror of my youth. Surely it was a hallucination, an ill-effect from the noxious fumes I had been inhaling from the time I entered this accursed house! I had to be imagining this, I thought as I reached for the knotted twine expecting the vision to disappear as soon as I reached for it. But NO! The wretched lasso was real, as I could tell from the coarse scrapings it left on the palm of my hand. I broke out in a cold sweat as the realizations of what was happening became abundantly clear. The horrid fairy tales of my youth were not a fantasy. They were REAL!

Mrs. Pines did murder her husband with a toxic poison. Bobby Robertson was tormented into a triple murder by his insane twin sisters. Eunice Berkhead had hung herself in the attic and suffered for days as the life slowly drained out of her. I could only assume the laboratory of Dr. Dencourt resided in the dreaded basement, but I was not about to venture there to find out.

I knew what I had to do. I was such a fool to think I was strong enough to conquer my fears. Why would I, Oliver Blackwell, be so arrogant that I could toss aside the existence of specters and apparitions and go about my life as an agnostic to all things paranormal? Who was I to ignore the desperate cries of those souls trapped in a world between the living and the dead and retell their stories as absurdist yarns? I must pay for my crimes against the poltergeists who inhabit this manor and I must do it now!

I reached up and grabbed the tattered rope and tugged on it to be sure it was secure. The noose hung from the center rafter and was as taut as the day it was fastened. I grabbed a chair that was eerily close to where I was standing, knocked to its side. Surely it was the chair Eunice Berkhead had used when she decided to take her own life. I positioned it under the hanging twine and steadied myself upon it. A little rickety it was, but stable enough to hold my weight. I seized the rope and placed it around my neck. With a quick jerk, I tightened it around my neck to be sure I wouldn't slip loose.

I kicked the chair from under me and quickly felt a crimp in my neck. The burly strands around my throat tightened and my airway became narrowed. I gasped for air and held tightly onto the twine that was constricting around me. My body jerked and convulsed as my lungs began to burn. I felt my last gasp of precious air was about to pass my lips when I heard a snap sound above my head. Before I could look up, I felt gravity take over my body and a terrifying free-fall began. My feet struck the rooted floor and quickly collapsed the splintered wood that was directly underneath me. My arms scraped against the thicket of fangs that the floorboards now resembled. I was falling fast down a shaft between the walls and floors, accumulating cobwebs, as my velocity seemed to accelerate. I could see whisps of light and shadow as my eyes caught glimpses of the second floor and first floor as they rushed past. My feet crashed through a flimsy rotted ceiling and my body smashed into the cold hard floor of the basement. I passed out for a second and when I gained consciousness I immediately felt a thousand pains shoot through my body. I looked down and saw that my leg was broken. My femur was sticking out of my calf and a large pool of blood was expanding underneath me. My left arm was shattered in two places and my right hand was crushed. My fingers resembled a mangled quagmire of flesh and bone. There were numerous shards of fractured timber penetrating every limb of my body and my breathing was labored from what I sensed were several broken ribs.

I was able to look around to gauge a sense of my surroundings. Small cracks of light beamed in from the area between the foundation and the frame of the house, illuminating what looked like some laboratory from another age. Test tubes and other analytical instruments were cluttered about the dank mold covered crypt. Was this the sanctum of the mad Dr. Dencourt? Of course it was! I knew now that the tall tales I told as a child were all rooted in fact not fiction. I was the only criminal now, for not believing the boding evil tales of terror. My crimes were ignorance and the self-affirming penalty was death! I could barely move as the cacophony of broken bones sent shockwaves of pain and torment throughout my body. My demise would be slow now. If there were only some way to hasten the passage to the other side. It was then that I saw it. Close by and within a grasp's reach—a rusty syringe. This could only be the trusty hypodermic needle of Dr. Dencourt, who I was beginning to think was not so mad after all, just misunderstood by the peons that refused to see his genius. I endured the pain as I crawled forward and grabbed the slender pointy cylinder of polished steel. It still had some liquid in it, and whether it was a cure-all or toxin I cared not. Injecting anything into my veins at this point would surely do me in. I jammed the needle into my arm with my good hand and injected myself with the rancid flaxen bisque that was contained within. My armed exploded with a fiery spasm that could only be described as hellish and agonizing. The sensation slowly made its way up my appendage and towards my heart. It wasn't long now before I would know what was on the other side of existence. I was glad I could pay penance for my blatant disregard for the warnings of the haunted spectral inhabitants of the house was soon to be my resting place. Would I now go on to be the subject of one of the grisly tales that was told at midnight campfire happenings and teenage sleepovers? I chuckled at the fact that I had become that of which I feared most. Soon my own spirit would haunt those brave enough to venture forth into the terrifying house that had no name. The house that took lives and enveloped souls. *The house at the end of the street.*

THE CONNECTION

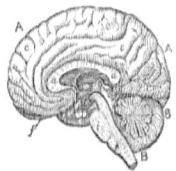

"I've created the perfect organism! After all these years I've finally done it!!" I threw my arms in the air, relishing in the grandeur of my success.

"Yes, doctor, you have done it, haven't you?"

The mocking voice of my adversary was quick to jab me with his sarcasm.

"But I wouldn't call it perfect," he added mordantly.

"Nonsense, it's flawless! I've astounded even myself with this brainchild! I must show it to the world!!"

His voice was quick to correct me, "I don't think they would like your creation, doctor."

"They couldn't accept it...the fools!!" I came back at him, "I would give the greatest discovery of modern science and still they would deem me a freak!"

"It's too bad that it had to turn out this way... if only you had thought about the consequences!"

"What consequences? I created it and I control it! Utterly and completely!"

"Don't get defensive, doctor, surely you realize something could go wrong!"

"Nothing can go wrong! My creation is perfect! PERFECT!!"

"Tsk, tsk! You don't want your blood pressure to rise...you do know what could happen if it did", he said condescendingly, "Don't you?"

I snapped: "My blood pressure is fine! Nothing can go wrong! All of the organs are carefully monitored!"

Again he was patronizing, "all the organs, doctor?"

I was becoming furious. "The heart, the lungs, the brain, everything is functioning perfectly!"

"The brain, doctor?" my adversary replied with an acerbic resonance that I could just taste. "How well have you been monitoring the brain?"

"The brain is monitored day and night. It was the most delicate part of the operation. The brain was difficult to remove—"

The bastard cut me off. "Which brain, doctor?"

"What?" I said pretending not to hear.

He repeated, "Which *brain,* doctor?"

"What are you saying?? There is only one!!" I had to correct him.

Still he persisted. "Which brain have you been monitoring, doctor??"

"There is only one brain!!" Was the mocker not listening?

"But there is *more* than one brain, doctor...don't you remember the operation...Don't you?... Doctor?!?"

The imbecile just wouldn't stop.

"You surgically grafted two brains together, doctor. Don't you remember how the monster screamed when you ripped open his skull?"

"No," I tried once more to educate the feeble-minded moron who persisted in accosting me, "The anesthesia worked fine!! There was no pain!!!"

"*I* seem to remember *the pain*, doctor!"

"There was NO PAIN!!!" I shrieked at him.

"Don't you remember the grotesque malformed head, doctor...of the monster with two brains??!"

Now, grudgingly, I had to concede his point.

"Of course I remember, you fool!! Don't mock me!! Can't you see the applications to modern science??"

I rose from the seat at my computer table. My blood burnt with indignation.

"Can't you see that a man with two brains will have twice the intelligence, work twice as fast and live twice as long?? CAN'T YOU?!!" I tried to remain adamant.

"No, doctor, the only thing I see is a man obsessed with his creation...his mad, twisted perversion of science, the perversion that was driving him insane!!" His voice had grown louder with outrage.

"YOU SIMPLETON!" I screamed at him at with the full force of my lungs, "You have only ever wanted to smother my accomplishments with your scorn and ridicule!"

"CONFESS, doctor, *YOU* are the monster with *TWO BRAINS!*"

"NO! I'm a genius, you fool!" I demanded the respect I deserved.

"A *genius?* Ha!...it was your twisted desire for glory that made you push beyond the boundaries of reason and morality... you *killed me* and *STOLE MY BRAIN!"*

Sickeningly, it dawned on me that the idiot, the idiot who had been taunting me, was the mocking voice was inside my own head.

"Then, using your own robot surgery, you grafted my brain onto yours. I don't know how you survived the transformation, but you did...you...we survived. You *SICK BASTARD*...what have you done to me??!!"

Still I wanted to argue--I improved your misbegotten life, I thought to myself.

"All I can remember is the pain...but that didn't matter to you, did it, doctor? All you cared about was your insane experiment...your mad journey into alchemy and bio-science...and you dragged me with you!!"

Revelations can shake the earth.

"And now, I'm here with you...inside your mind! I'm constantly subjected to your perverted fantasies...your twisted desires...I can never escape, I can never make it stop!"

Ah, that is *true, so true.*

"And now, I can feel your brain...it's stronger...it's taking over..."

As it should be.

"Soon your brain will dominate mine...I will be nothing."

No matter how much he whined, he was soon to be a footnote in the annals of science.

"But I'm not going to let that happen, doctor..."

A loud crash from the operating tables behind me made me turn around. The horrid monstrosity that stood there before me was loathsome, vile beyond comprehension. The human carcass, whose extracted cranial organ I had grafted onto mine, was stumbling towards me. His skull was as I'd left it, gaping, exposed at the top, empty with nothing to control the lumbering frame beneath. Yet, its hideous form continued forward, moving towards me, the focus of all its hate and resentment. With nowhere to go I could only retreat. Weak and still recuperating from the operation, I knew I could not defend myself.

Backing up, some liquid on the floor caught my eye. In its yellowish green surface I saw a reflection of myself. The man I had been was no more. In fact, I was no longer a man at all—in his place there was only a maniacal looking creature with an oversized and deformed cranium. My head, grotesque and twisted, was now the home of *two* encephalopathy organs instead of one. The ripples in the rancid goop on the floor, reflecting and distorting my image, foreshadowed what was to come.

The abhorrent behemoth before me was clutching a large blade in his hand, one I had used for cutting through the thick hides of animals and the largest of bones. As I backed myself into a corner, I knew this was the end. My ill-fated obsession with the darkest reaches of science had been my undoing.

As the thing raised its weapon and plunged it deep into my

skull the last words I heard were…

"I WANT MY BRAIN BACK!"

THE SLEEPING ONE

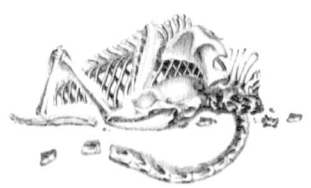

The most merciful thing in the world, I think, is the inability of the human mind to correlate all its contents. We live on a placid island of ignorance in the midst of black seas of infinity, and it was not meant that we should voyage far. The sciences, each straining in its own direction, have hitherto harmed us little; but some day the piecing together of dissociated knowledge will open up such terrifying vistas of reality, and of our frightful position therein, that we shall either go mad from the revelation or flee from the deadly light into the peace and safety of a new dark age. Howard Phillips Lovecraft "<u>The Call of Cthulhu</u>" August or September 1926

I did not expect to find much work when I traveled to the port town of Rileh, Massachusetts, for its population was just under one thousand residents. However, with my debts piled up and the inability to generate wealth on a consistent basis, I was left with no choice. Ironically, my move away from the big city to this small, run-down town filled with miserable-looking fellows proved to be much more profitable. As luck would have it (not for them of course) they had been lacking a veterinarian for quite some time. So, imagine my surprise at the influx of feline, canine, and even some Aquarian pets brought to my doorstep for treatment.

Now, the residents of Rileh were not affluent at all, but they did pay what they could for treatment, as they loved their less-intelligent and furry companions. Much more so than the folks did back in the more densely popular areas. Looking back on it, it was rather obvious. The citizens of Rileh seemed to be much more simplistic, allowing them to be more in tune with their environment and sought to protect it. While I am all for the preservation of animal life and the conservation of resources, these folks took it to a far more religious place.

With that said, it is not at all astonishing that they would call upon me to handle an obscure case of nature. It was on the fourth day of October 1910, on a frigid and foggy morning that the town pastor rapped his hand aggressively against my door to rouse me from a deep sleep. Groggily, I put on a pair of slacks and added a tie to my shirt in order to make my disheveled self look slightly more presentable. Donning a jacket, I opened the door and was met with a deeply concerned looking pastor. His hair was matted from sweat and part of his shirt was not tucked into his pants. I nearly chuckled, thinking to myself he had been defrocked from his position, alas that was not the reason for his appearance at my door.

"Nathaniel! Come; make haste with me to the beach. Something has washed up on the shore and requires your assistance in identifying the creature." I shrugged at his insistence and told the man to relax that it must be some beached whale or other aquatic animals that met an early and unfortunate end. "Oh no, Nathaniel. This is nothing of the sort! Please, I implore you. You have served our community well, if it is a matter of payment we shall pay the price." He had my attention now, I had a debtor who was coming in the next week and I was short on the payment, so I finally acquiesced to his pleas.

"Very well, lead the way pastor." Together we ran through the stale and freezing air, my lungs burning from the cold. Ten minutes later we finally arrived at the scene and I could see a large crowd huddling together like a pack of wildebeests for warmth. Even from a distance, I could hear them 'ooing' and 'ahhing' at something that their bodies had hidden from my view.

"There! Doctor Nathaniel is here, make way!" One of the boys, whose dog I had treated the day before for worms had shouted, alerting everyone else to my presence. I found the whole situation unsettling, to say the least. It was extraordinarily rare to see the folks of this sleepy-town be so active and excited about anything.

The crowd then parted for me as though I were Moses parting the waves and pointed me in the direction of the peculiarity that the green-blue waves were nudging up against. Before I could begin my walk, the pastor grabbed me by the arm and whispered a warning into my ear.

"Care, Nathaniel. Take your steps wisely." Bemused by this, I merely nodded, unsure if the warning was nefarious with intent or not, and continued my brief walk over to the specimen to be examined.

As soon as my eyes rested on the disturbing and incredulously large scaly and slimy looking creature, I visibly recoiled backward, letting out a 'gah!' Much to my chagrin as it amused the bystanders to see me rattled. Once I composed myself, I immediately lost my poise once the odor of the marine-beast and its decay snaked its way into my nostrils. I gagged and covered my face with my jacket sleeve as I approached the unknown entity after much encouragement from the town.

Looking over the monstrous form in front of me, I estimated it to be around thirty feet from end to end. As for its body, it was indeed covered in scales but had many pores from which black-talon like appendages sprouted from. Amazingly enough, the oceanic-creature did not resemble any other marine life that I could recognize, save for a few details which I will relay shortly.

Overall, the creature resembled a man to a certain extent. Namely due to the behemoth being bipedal. It had enormous and thick muscular legs, covered with not only the spikes described above but also tendrils as well from random orifices. Also, what appeared to be feet were both webbed and clawed, bewildered, and intrigued the vet in me. Moving on to its head, it looked like the head of an octopus had been sliced off and grafted onto the neck of a human, creating a twisted homunculus.

In the end, I had a single iota of an idea as to what the thing was, but I was not about to say so in front of nearly the entire town.

"I will need tents set up to cover this creature as I require privacy. I intend to dissect this curiosity from the sea. Any able man, I implore you to help me in this matter for we are on the verge of great scientific discoveries!" I said using the best showmanship voice I could muster.

"And to see how we may better protect the life that exists within our harbors!" Someone from the crowd called out, which received much more applause than the declaration I had made. Either way, it was nice to see the town so enthused about something for once, so I applauded along.

The strongmen of Rileh then lent me their arms and so we constructed a perimeter around the dead hellion-spawn and erected drab grey tents above it. I thanked the gentleman and offered to show my thanks with a meal, but they declined, saying 'we are happy with the work you will do, that is payment enough.' I gave an awkward smile and turned to the monstrous creature before me, giving it a look over again before donning my smock, gloves, and mask.

Taking a scalpel, I determined to start with its cranium; a rather daunting task considering it was easily quadrupled in size to my own. I chuckled at the absurdity of my small knife being able to cut into the massive head. But, I found a great surprise in how easily the blade slipped beneath the skin and opened up the gelatinous flesh. I made great progress but my blade was paused by the thick durability of the skull. Opting for a hammer, I aimed it at the exposed cranium and brought it down with great force, hearing it crack beneath the metal.

However, after setting aside the hammer and before I could look inside of the questionable creature, a cloud of green mist poured out from the hole and I could not prevent a portion of it from invading my nose and filling my senses. Immediately, nausea overcame me and my stomach flipped onto its side, bracing for the worse I aimed for the sand to empty the contents of bowels. Only, nothing came, and instead of vacating the sour liquids within me, a cutting headache scraped up my brain. My vision blurred and turned white as rapid images of an enormous and draconic creature mixed with an octopod-like beast flew amongst the stars and lay waste to nations. And then, blackness.

"Heavens above!" I shouted as I regained consciousness. Rapidly, I looked around and saw that night had fallen on the dreadful town of Rileh. I sat up, wiping cool sand off of myself before looking at the huge frame of the creature in front of me. Deeply perturbed by the mad images I had seen, I scampered away like a frightened child and walked with a quick pace back to my home.

I then bathed, trying to wash away the grime and the smell of death off my body and to cleanse my mind of the ungodly things I had seen when I fell comatose. After draining the tub and getting dressed for bed, I heard a pair of hands knock one after another at my door. I looked through the peephole of my door and saw that the pastor had returned with a man I had not yet seen before in town. Opening the door, I greeted the men and asked what I could do for them at this late hour.

"Mr. Nathtaniel, please, tell us what you have learned from your autopsy today. Mr. Gracefield and I simply can not wait to hear about it." I look at the skinny yet tall man next to the pastor. His eyes were sunken and dark, prominent cheekbones due to his thin frame, and had on a large robe that I likened monastery monks would wear. I thought perhaps he wore it to defend his body from the chilly elements that were coming more and more each day.

"Pastor, I...I am not ready to disclose what I have discovered. Now if you excuse me-" I started to say, closing the door but was stopped by Mr. Gracefield forcefully keeping the door open.

"You, you saw something did you not? Yes...yes it is written on your face! I can see that you have been 'touched' and implanted with knowledge few men could comprehend! Do share it with us!" A wild and desperate look spread across his face and I could feel how deeply his curiosity had been aroused. Put off by the two men, I ignored what they side and slammed the door in their faces.

"All is well Mr. Nathaniel!" The pastor said from the other side of the door. "Over time we are sure that you will comply and share the wonderful things that you have been made cognizant of. Goodnight dear sir." I looked through my peephole and saw the men walk away. I quickly locked my door and put a chair beneath the handle in order to make myself feel safe.

"Freaks and abnormal are what they are, I'd never have guessed the pastor would be friends with a man such as thought." Sighing, I shook my head and climbed into bed quite fatigued and with my headache returning. In spite of the weirdness of the day, sleep closed my eyes and sent me under.

Rather than having a night of peaceful rest free from more anxiety-inducing events, I dreamed of things that I knew for a fact that man should never be made privy to. Within these dreams, I was but a soul, a third-person observer if you will, under the vast oceans. My vision dove far away from the light of the surface and into the black abyss. For some reason or another, I was graced with being able to see without the aid of light, which I realize was more of a curse than anything.

Below me, under the crushing weight of the ocean was a colossal city made of stone crafted with intricate precision. It was remarkable how resilient the city was to the erosion of the water around it, yet at the same time, I felt incredibly apprehensive being near it. Especially the statue of an enormous goliath creature that resembled the beast that was washed up on the shore of Rileh. Only, this one, in particular, was no doubt akin to a king to it, for why else would a statue be built in its honor?

Observing the gargantuan statue brought me no feeling of safety, security, or awe, only a foreboding sense of dread. My consciousness then drifted further towards it and I saw innumerable amounts of those miniature versions of it swimming around erratically. I thanked my stars that I was seemingly not able to be seen by those worshipping sentries.

Watching them flail and swim about in the water was alarming, to say the least. Worst of all the one that had washed up on the shore was nothing compared to the chilling size of those found here. As a matter of fact, a couple was around half the size of the statue itself. Only with one main difference between the two: despite being stationary, the alien god-like creature that sat in the center of them exuded an amount of a malevolence that no mortal creature could match.

Finally, after drifting closer I now found myself face to face with the octopoid head of the beast and came to a horrifying realization; what lay before me was not the creation of brass, steel or stone. The behemoth in front of me was organic, made from a substance most likely unearthly and deeply profane, as the water around it seemed to be slightly repelled by its very existence.

I do not know how it managed to stay completely still and unbothered by the insane amount of pressure that was found at the bottom of the seafloor. But then, the tentacles protruding from its face twitched. Its wings flicked up slightly and its massive body flexed its muscles, shoving the water around it outward from that alone. And then, by God above, it opened its eyes. Those ruby-colored eyes shone brightly in the abyss of darkness like hellfire.

All of its followers picked up their speed and swarmed around their king rapidly with demented excitement as it began to stand up. Although, right as it pulled its wings back and flexed them in order to propel itself up to the surface, its eyes locked with me. I could not look away from its piercing gaze and begin to panic. Even though I was nothing but a specter observing these events I could feel my physical body seize up and fall under some sort of spell. However, as the great and ancient beast began its approach towards me, I was thankfully roused from my slumber.

Sitting up in my body, I was covered in a thick and foul-smelling green layer of slime that must have come from my pores instead of sweat. In disgust, I quickly wiped away the gross and unknown substance off of my person and promptly started a bath. Not wanting to deal with the bedclothes of mine that were drenched in the filthy substance, I tossed it out of my window. After my bath, I saw the sun was beginning to rise but instead of feeling joyous for the start of a new day, I was drawn to the ocean.

My vision blurred and words from an unknown language poured out from my mouth. When I came to my senses due to a few birds chirping wildly outside of my door, one word stuck out to me: Cthulhu. The memory of that word in particular and the others I could not remember left a sour taste in my mouth and sharp pains shot through my brain. It was there that I connected the word with what I saw in my vision, and it was a realization that I could not deny. The word was not a word, but rather a name and it must have been the name of that terrifying creature that slept beneath the waves of the world. Or it could be the name of its followers, but the former is far more probable and much more disquieting.

After getting dressed, I trudged back towards the tented area where the corpse of the monster I was to continue dissecting remained. Only, when I donned my mask and entered the tents, I found the pastor alongside his odd friend there waiting for me. What was not waiting for me however was the beast. It was gone and all that remained was a dark imprint in the sand and various foul-smelling liquids. And what did I spy in the hands of Mr. Gracefield? The clothes covered in gelatinous slime I had tossed out only two hours before.

"What is going on here?" I demanded, yet not truly wanting to know the answer to my question.

"This is all the evidence we need Mr. Nathaniel! You have been chosen by the Great Old One! He Who Dreams has selected you for a grandiose task that only you and a select other few can accomplish. Now, come hither Mr. Nathaniel so you can begin your next step!" I did not say a word in response to this nonsense and started to run away but was caught by two burly and stern-looking policemen. I yelled at them to unhand me but my efforts were in vain, I knew none would come to my rescue and resigned myself to whatever fate awaited me.

Mr. Gracefield then draped the slime-covered bedclothes of mine over my head and on the shirt wrote some crude signs onto it with a fountain pen. I was then escorted to where the waves met the sand and heard as he chanted aloud.

"R'lyeh ghiofh mgilfh Rng'ulgh Cthulhu!" And then shoved a palm of his against my left ribcage and then told all of the men to leave me alone. Thinking I was free to run, I turned to dart away but could not move. Or rather, my body did not want to run, instead I was pulled to the ocean. And despite my mental protests, my legs trudged one step at a time, going deeper and deeper into the water. I felt my head expand and tendrils burst out from my chin and my skin became a sickly-green and covered in scales. Soon, all I could hear was the call of my king, who beckoned me to his city.

"Do you believe he shall awaken the One Who Sleeps?" The pastor asked Mr. Gracefield.

"Only if the stars are right, pastor. Only if they are right." The cultist said as they saw the newly transformed spawn of the Great Old One dive down into the murky waters.

We watched the waves subside as the thing disappeared into the depths. I could only wonder if there were more of these hell-spawned beasts being born or hatched below the waves. Underneath the muck, where light doesn't go, where the darkness is so profoundly black only evil and wickedness are allowed; this is where the thing called Cthulhu dwells.

I realized that humanity was only allowed to live here on this Earth, given permission by the colossal gods and monsters that once ruled its grounds. How long, I wondered, before these demonic gargantuan beasts will want to take it back.

We are only here until they decide it's time for us to go.

SHOCKING TERRORS #13

I had read many a strange tale in the musty used horror pulps of the 1930s and 40s, but nothing came close to the utter terror I experienced when reading a piece of short fiction from the pages of *Shocking Terrors* #13.

As a teen, I stayed awake many nights reading with my flashlight under my covers, tales of unspeakable weirdness, bloodthirsty demons and maniacal mad doctors, and they always gave me a shiver. That adrenal rush I got when reading bizarre descriptions of abhorrent creatures or the twist shock ending that you never saw coming was what I sought again and again. In the pages of pulp science fiction and horror mags of yesteryear is where I found it.

My youth was spent mainly alone. My father worked long hours and my mother, a housewife, was always preoccupied with her daily soap operas and romance novels. I had a few close friends, who would be considered nerds or geeks, who'd spend weekends enacting role-playing games like *Dungeons and Dragons* or *Attack of the Zombie Mutants*. When we weren't throwing twenty-sided dice around, we could be found devouring comic books or black and white horror mags like *Eerie* and *Creepy*. We liked those as every once in a while you would be able to see a nude woman or bare breast in the cheap newsprint pages. I was always a fan of Heavy Metal, as it was not shy about placing graphic erotica stories in between its staple of European Sci-fi and horror tales.

Sports and other physical activities would take a back seat for my friends and I, unless we were dressed up as medieval knights doing battle in the most anachronistic way we could. A library basement, where the used sci-fi books would be sold for ten cents or a comic book convention would be where we spent our weekends, never at the high school football or baseball game.

My friend Jerry was similar to me as he liked graphic fiction and had a huge collection of vintage comics, many of which were preserved in plastic bags and archival backing boards, in hopes of selling them in the future as their value rose to sky-high values. Other comics, worn and musty, their spines weak and rolled from countless page turns and collector trades, were devoured by us for their graphic stories of super-humans and dastardly villains. These comics were aptly named "readers" as we could do just that without fear of degrading the value of the pictorial periodical.

Tom, the third misfit in our gang, more of a film aficionado, and spent his time collecting old 8mm and 16mm films, with less of the latter as they were more expensive. Tom's income could not keep up with the more costly collectibles, so he went for quantity over quality. He filled the void with the accumulation of VHS tapes of low-budget horror and sci-fi films, which were mainly purchased for their lavish illustrated covers than for the films themselves.

For me it was the pulps. It was *always* the pulps. That's what I collected. They had these amazing painted covers by the top illustrators of the day that drew you right in. Their interiors were peppered with black and white spot illustrations by other artisans who specialized in brush and quill line work. They were masters of light and shadow. In the back of the mags were many reviews of other books and periodicals of the day, which would lead me on other exciting quests for even more treasures of sensational fiction. Further in the back pages were ads for the sales of used magazines, or sign-ups for fiction-fan clubs where like-minded fans could meet up or calk it up with pen pals, discussing their favorite authors and stories of the day.

Many a weekend I would spend in a used bookstore flipping through boxes in search of rare issues of *Astounding Science Fiction, Weird Tales* or *Bizarre Fantasy Worlds* in search of the cover illo that would make my heart skip a beat.

Issues like *Amazing Stories*, the August 1927 issue, featuring the metallic alien creatures attacking the earth from an H.G. Wells' *War of the Worlds* saga. Or what sci-fi geek's collection would be complete without *Thrilling Wonder Stories*, April 1949, with its exquisitely painted cover of a scantily clad princess about to be accosted by a troop of laser gun wielding Martians. Or what about *Fantastic Universe*, Feb. 1954, with it depiction of a spaceman discovering his skeletonized comrade on a distant planet while malevolent UFOs approach from the skies, insuring his doom.

Amazing Fiction #27, May 1954, a hard to find edition that had eluded me for years, was found in the back of a twenty-five cent bin at a lower end sci-fi con. Its cover of a flying saucer doing battle with a rocket ship that clearly had the emblem of the U.S. flag on its side. Looking closely at the U.F.O. one could discern a U.S.S.R. star and crescent logo on its shiny exterior. This issue was a Cold War relic for sure.

A rare find indeed was *Famous Fantastic Mysteries*, August 1946, whose cover, at first glance depicted the illusion of a greenish skull, only upon closer examination one could discern the almost nude bodies of men and women entangled in what could only be described as a sex orgy. I was sure this issue had been banned in some states for this image, but I could not be sure.

Aside from the covers, the real reason I collected these mags was for the fiction. Robert E. Howard, August Derleth and R.R. Nicholson were among the authors who were my favorites, as they were for most of the readers. But being a consumer of all sorts of science and horror fiction, I also sought out many of the lesser known writers, as they may not have made a name for themselves, but were of equal or even better quality than those aforementioned dignitaries of the genre. It was sad that these narrative craftsmen would soon be lost to time and space just like one of their doomed protagonists in one of their short stores. Many of these short tales were not collected into hardbound or paperback anthologies by the larger publishers, as these lesser-known names did not sell the quantities to justify even a small print run. It was the possible discovery of these rare pieces of unknown fiction that got me out of bed in the morning.

Anyone could find the complete collection of R.R. Nicholson, as they were in the public domain and reprinted by numerous publishers over the years. Even his letters, poems and notebooks were printed, bound and distributed all over the world.

But it was writers like J.L. Dmitri, whose *Tales of Necromancy and Demons* were written in a prose that was way ahead of his time, that really jumped off the page like no other. Edmond Quinn had scribed tales so dark and disturbing they were banned in seven countries when published in the late 30s.

Sadly, because these writers loved the science fiction and horror genres, the only home they could find for their tales was in the pages of the much-derived pulps. The simple-mined literature critics of the day had largely ignored these writers, or when they did write a review of a particular story, they would sneer over their use of adjectives and strange sentence structures. These cavalier judges deemed these craftsmen hacks, while I marveled at their rejection of punctuation and creative uses of verbs and predicates.

Who could forget the great Xavier Clark, a pseudonym for a woman writer who would have been laughed out of the sci-fi men's club even they even had a hint of her gender. Xavier, or Dr. Linda Farewell as she was named at birth, crafted tales of bizarre fantasies on alien worlds where leather clad swordsmen shared the battlefields with fierce amazon warriors who were easily their match when sword clashed against sword. Amazingly, no one ever suspected Xavier was really of the feminine persuasion, but to me it was right there on the page as many of her stories featured female protagonists who constantly defeated their weaker male adversaries in combat.

Even the Asimov-award winning writer Basset Hamilton described Xavier Clark as one of the best writers in the business and that *he* should be celebrated more often at sci-fi cons and book signings. *It was too bad* he lamented that poor Xavier would have to be an agoraphobic and be confined to his typewriter for months on end. Little did Mr. Hamilton know, that Xavier Clark's alter ego was a high ranking English literature professor at Yale University. If the ivy-league school ever found out one of their top faculty members was slumming around in the pulps, it would surely be an embarrassment to the facility. An incident Dr. Linda Farewell was not about to be exposed to, the paltry sum she received for the pulp writings was not enough for her to quit her tenured position. In later diary entries, Dr. Farewell said he was amused at how the science fiction and horror boys club *marveled* at her writings and place her work high on a pedestal. To her it was a fun hobby to be the secretive scribe playing in the realm of lurid fantasy myth creation.

That said, no writer was more sought after than Fitzgerald Moore. A true master of his craft, Fitzgerald wove tales of demonic possession and ghastly apparitions that would turns ones stomach and twist your brain should you even be able to finish one of his tales. Dejectedly, his stories never graced the pages of *Weird Fantasy* or *Amazing Stories*; he was relegated to lesser pulp mags like *Terror Tales* and *Haunted Horrors*. These smaller zines were sometimes not distributed on newsstands and available by subscription only, even further reducing his fan base and exposure. This also meant that these magazines had lower print runs and over the decades, less of them survived, making them more rare and sought after by collectors like me.

With Fitzgerald Moore, there were only two published stories known to exist with a third tale only rumored to have been published. "The Doom That Came From Space" was the featured story on *Haunted Horrors* #3, May 1946, and told the tale of a horrific virus that emerged from a crashed meteor and enveloped a town and later the entire Earth, causing hallucinations, insanity and cannibalism to all who came in contact with it.

"The Strange Case of Ridley Johns", published in *Terror Tales* #9, August 1947, was a morbid story of Satanism, possession and suicidal death. Various other pulp writers gave high praise to the tale, but some fans were so repulsed by its content they vowed never to read another Fitzgerald Moore yarn as long as they lived.

The hidden fact about Moore was that no one even knew he was a black man. Should the white Anglo-American science fiction gatekeepers even suspected Moore's race, they would have surely shunned him and his work forever. One could tell of these writer's white supremacist views from their personal letters, which had survived the decades. Now not all of them held these racist views, but even the one's that didn't maintained a crude silence as to not offend their peers. Even though many of the top writers were Jewish, they had changed their names and faked their religion as it was the high time of Nazi and Soviet oppression in the 1930s-40s. These writers had good reason to stay in the shadows, as even in the United States there was widespread bigotry against many races from white America.

In any case not much of Fitzgerald Moore was known other than he was a slightly secretive person who lived in solitary somewhere in the mid-west. He wrote only those two stories that we know about and may have made his living writing under various pseudonyms crafting romance, mystery and thriller novels for various other publishers.

Now, one would be satisfied with these two stories by Fitzgerald Moore, as they were so good, it was speculated that he stopped because he feared he could never top the suspenseful terror he created therein. Rumors abounded that there was a third tale written, maybe published maybe not, that existed somewhere out there in the wilds of the pulp wasteland. Once I heard about this fabled lost tale, I made it my sole purpose of being to find it.

For years I searched through the used books bins at conventions and bookstores only to come up empty handed with anything relating to this third lost tale. If it weren't for my obsession with reading the back pages of these fiction mags I would never have come across any proof of its existence. It was one day; I was skimming through the classified ad pages in the back of *Strange Mystery Tales* #77 that I came across the mention of the lost tale by Fitzgerald Moore. A story so dreadful and terrifying that all recorded copies of its existence had been burned or destroyed.

The rare issue that this story had appeared in was the elusive *Shocking Terrors* #13. A want ad, in the back of *Strange Mystery Tales* #77, explicitly stated he was looking for a copy of *Shocking Terrors* #13, in any condition and price was no object.

I immediately went to a few confidant collectors and asked them about the seldom seen *Shocking Terrors* #13. To my surprise, most of them had heard of the issue, but never actually seen a copy and for all intent and purposes, the existence of the issue was just a rumor. There were a few rare book dealers that insisted the issue was real, but it was so hard to find, the rumor was that there might only be one copy that survived. *Survived what?* I wondered.

I listened intently as this one rare book dealer, now maybe in his late 70s, told me the story of Fitzgerald's third tale, a horrific narrative so disturbing that all copies had been burned or destroyed and that maybe, just maybe, one copy had made it out alive. There were stories of readers who dared gaze upon the bewitched words, had soon met a terrible demise. Some readers of the "third tale" had gone insane before even getting to the end. Other horror savants suffered terrible illnesses by themselves or their close family members. These fables had been passed down through the generations of pulp readers and dealers and had largely been forgotten by all but a few dedicated horror fiction aficionados. I suspected that, between the decades and generations of ear-to-mouth passage, these stories gained appalling details and added hideous demises as they went.

Not one to believe in specters and possession, I would not be afraid to gaze upon the elusive tale, should I be lucky enough to find the rare issue. The paranormal occultists and the agnostic skeptics have long debated the possibility of the demonic possession of artifacts. Even in our role-playing games, we would entertain the notion of ancient artifacts that were possessed by demonic spirits. Many a horror tale was told that involved a bedeviled amulet or rune-staff whose power corrupted the greedy. These were enthralling story devices, but I did not believe them to be real, not for an instant. One could easily be taken in by superstitions and I was acutely aware of the absurdity of the notion of a Pulp-fiction magazine being somehow possessed by a malignant spirit or curse.

So my quest for the rare issue of *Shocking Terrors* had begun. Scouring the back pages of the pulps for more proof of its existence, I chanced upon an article in the back of *Analog Science Fiction*, the Oct. 1969 issue. A reviewer named Thom Busiek had come upon the lost issue of *Shocking Terrors* #13 and read Fitzgerald Moore's said story and described it as the most terrifying words ever written.

Then a month later in *Analog Science Fiction*, the Nov. 1969 issue, there was an obituary, a rarity for these sci-fi rags that listed Thom Busiek as deceased from a recent unknown illness. It listed his credits as a reviewer and sometimes writer of fiction and that was it.

Another review of *Shocking Terrors* #13 I found was in the back of *Astonishing Science Fiction* #45, by a man named John who described the tales as horrid and frightening and the reader found himself unable to sleep for days afterwards. I could not find any Obit of this writer in following issues, but no reviews by him were ever published again, at least in the pages of *Astonishing Science Fiction.*

I managed to acquire copies of *Shocking Terrors* #12 and *Shocking Terrors* #14 at a local used bookstore. *Shocking Terrors* #15 seemed to be the last issue ever printed, published Spring 1954, which I found from a mail order catalog out of Sacramento, CA.

My research discovered that *Shocking Terrors* was a subscription only magazine and print runs were mostly under 500 copies, at least according to the pulp aficionados who were "in the know". No official records were ever kept or published, but I do know that any issue of *Shocking Terrors* was extremely hard to find with #13 being the elusive to the point of people wondering if it ever existed at all. With no one ever even seeing the cover, or being able to describe it, rumors also abounded that the publisher, being of the superstitious lot, has skipped issue 13 all together much like a hotel or apartment building would skip the 13th floor. Apprehensive patrons are unlikely to stay or live on the floor with the unlucky number.

I searched, but could not find the whereabouts of the publisher of *Shocking Terrors*, a man named Caleb Johnston, who seemed to be based out of Akron, Ohio for the full run of the magazine. The mailing address was a P.O. Box in Akron, that had been abandoned long ago, and the building that the post office resided in had also been demolished. I had done a little digging about some of the authors featured in the mag, hoping some may still be alive, but I came up with nothing. Any letters I had written to old addresses I had found and been returned to me "undeliverable". No one else in the pulp circuit seemed to have any connection to anyone else in the magazine, and having ceased publication over 30 years ago, it seemed feasible, that no connections to the contributors could be made. The inner workings of a self-published underground sci-fi pulp was not going to be on the radar of anyone except the most hard core of fans.

The Annual Baltimore Sci-Fi Pulp Con was fast approaching and all of the big dealers were going to be there. I didn't want t alert anyone that I was on the lookout for *Shocking Terrors* #13, as there would surely be some fraudster who would try and pawn off a bootleg copy to me for several hundred dollars. Seeing that no one knew what the cover looked like, one could easily be duped. I thought it was best to keep a low profile and just search through the boxes of used titles in hopes of finding a copy by chance. Sometimes dealers would buy a large collection of pulps from an estate sale, and in his haste to flip the mags for a quick buck, would neglect to go through each and every copy looking for rare or key issues or mint condition firsts. You'd think something like this wouldn't happen, but it did. There were so many magazines being traded and sold at shows, sometimes whole collections were traded three and four times in a single day with a 20% mark-up each time it changed hands.

Money could be made hand over fist quite quickly. Some dealers were just in it for the profit and not into reading the magazines at all. Such a shame, I would think, all that time spent buying and selling vintage science fiction and never opening the pages to indulge and marvel at what was inside. To each his own, I would carry on, at least I was able to enjoy a full and imaginative past-time by delving into the fanciful worlds of robots, spaceships, demons and loathsome horrors from deep space.

While I did delve into reading science fiction, I was always more partial to horror. This is why magazines like *Eerie Stories, Strange Tales* and *Shocking Terrors* always spoke to me. There seemed to be a ten to one ratio of sci-fi mags to horror, but that was fine with me, as I had over seventy years of classic pulp terror tales to find as a dug through old book bins and cardboard boxes.

I arrived at *The Annual Baltimore Sci-Fi Pulp Con* bright and early and bought a $15 pass to get into the convention thirty minutes early to go through the tables. I recognized many of the dealers, but there were some I hadn't seen before. The first table I spotted had a huge collection of *Ghost Stories* and *Uncanny Tales*, of which I already had many. The second table seemed to have more copies of *Mystery Thrillers* and *Argosy* along with some vintage sci-fi comics.

I made my way down the aisle and spotted the table for Jim's Pulps, a rare book dealer out of New York.

"Anything new?" I asked.

"Just picked up a collection out of Rhode Island, check that box there." Jim pointed at a white cardboard box that seemed to have exactly what I was looking for.

"Thanks," I replied and began flipping through the musty bound newsprint. *Weird Tales, The Spirit, Men's Adventure Stories* and *Fantastic Mysteries* seemed to fill out the box.

"Any rare horror pulps?" I asked trying to not look too desperate.

"Mostly sci-fi here, try Book Broker a few aisles down." And I did exactly that.

Book broker had been in the game for a while, and their booth was double the size of most. They had it all, comics, pulps, art books, and rare hardcovers. I began looking through the bins when one of the booth guys came over to me.

"Looking for anything in particular?" he said with a smile, trying to size me up.

"Looking for underground horror pulps, y'know the kind that no one else wants," I wanted to let him think I was a cheapskate.

"Oh, sure, there's a dollar box over there, but if you want some really rare stuff, check that box up front."

Now I had to check both. I flipped through the dollar box and came up empty, so quickly moved over to the more expensive box. These were nicely bagged and boarded copies of *Astounding Fantasy, Morbid Tales* and *Fantastic Adventure*. A nice lot, but I didn't think my rare item was going to be found here.

While flipping through the mags I always had an ear out for the conversations going on around me. You could hear fans and dealers discussing a rare cover of *Planet Stories* or how they recently picked up a mint edition of *Future Science Fiction #1* from a man whose grandfather died and they didn't know what they had. Everyone was so excited to be there, you could feel the excitement for vintage fiction emanating throughout the room.

It was then that I heard it. Two older gentlemen, one overweight and both wearing black over worn t-shirts that sported images of horror or tights and capes wearing heroes.

"I've been on the lookout for *Shocking Terrors* #13," the smaller one said in hushed tones.

"Ha! That books only a rumor," replied the larger man.

I stopped shuffling through the magazines and listened intently to what they were saying.

"Oh, it's real. It's *very* real," the believer kept on.

"You're on a fool's quest my friend, that issue is a folk tale. No one's ever seen or even had possession of it. The copies I've seen are bootleg, " the skeptic persisted.

"You're a non-believer, I see. I'm telling you the issue exists! And I've heard from a few dealers it might be here at this very con."

Could it be? I thought to myself.

"If you want to spend your days looking for some supposedly "cursed" pulp magazine, be my guest," the skeptic was not convinced.

"I'm telling you, it's here, and I can feel it."

The men walked past.

That was all I needed to add fuel to my quest. Not only was there a great possibility of this rarely, if ever, issue was here, but there were other hunters looking for it. I had to be diligent in my search. I was not going to let some speculator, or part-time fiction fan beat me to my prize.

I quickly looked through the remaining books on the table I was at and move quickly to the next.

I didn't want to give away what I was looking for, or the amount I wanted to pay but I had to quicken my pace. I sized up the seller at the next booth; he seemed honest enough, as I listened in on his interaction with the patron he was talking to. His merchandise was not overpriced and he had a fair selection of sci-fi and horror, with just a dabbling of crime. I surmised he would have some knowledge of the book I was looking for.

"Hey," I said to the dealer at John's Book Nook, "I'm looking for a rare science fiction pulp."

"We got all kinds here," he graciously replied, "what's your poison?"

I leaned in and under my breath whispered, *"Shocking Terrors #13."*

His eyebrow raised. He didn't seem stunned or bewildered.

"A rare book indeed," he replied.

"So, have you ever come across one?"

"No, but I do believe it's out there. Maybe not a lot of copies, it's said that they were all burned or destroyed. You've heard the rumors I take it?"

He motioned for me to come behind his table. I could see he had something to tell me, but wanted to do it in private.

"Yes, the book is cursed, all those who read it meet an untimely death. I don't believe in all that. I'm just trying to complete my collection, I have the other two Fitzgerald Moore stories, an I'm trying to get my hands on the third."

"A completest, eh?" I hear you, I was like that with *Fantastic Stories*, took me fifteen years, but I have the entire run."

"I have most of them as well."

"A great series, amazing covers."

"I get them mostly for the stories," we were getting off-track.

"As for *Shocking Terrors* #13, I would beware of that issue."

"What do you mean?"

"I think there might be some truth to the fables."

"You mean the supposed curse?"

"Things can be possessed by evil, just as people can, and I think that book is one of them."

"Well, I feel it's all just rumor. Tales that have been spun and exaggerated over time seem to become urban legends that everyone believes. I'm not convinced."

"I've been in this game a long time and every few years I see someone like you, hearing the legends of *Shocking Terrors* #13 and they sometimes spend years in hot pursuit of the mythical tome, " he paused, "Don't let the obsession with pirate treasure get the best of you."

Thanks for the warning, " I replied, "So you've never come across a copy I take it?"

"Not personally."

"But you know someone who has?"

He hesitated, looked around to see if anyone was listening. "I have."

My heart raced. This was the first time anyone had ever even admitted to knowing someone who had come in contact with the scarce issue.

"I'm listening," I egged him on.

"It was about ten years ago, a customer of mine, very similar to you, had heard the tales and became obsessed with finding the same book you seek. His search led him to a man in Detroit who had a huge collection of pulps. He claimed to have the very issue, *Shocking Terrors* #13. The dealer claimed he never read the book, but picked it up in an estate sale and just kept it safe and hidden, in hopes of letting the value increase, and one day selling it. As he heard more about its possessed nature, the man decided it was in his best interests to hold the book and keep it safe from the world."

"And the man looking for it?"

"As it turned out, the dealer came into some tough times, some health problems caused him to have to liquidate his entire estate and stock of books, and *Shocking Terrors* #13 was one of the last books in his collection."

"Are you implying that the dealer's affliction was connected to the book?"

"My personal feeling is that just having the book in one's possession is enough to cause ill-effects, not to mention reading it."

I had to admit; this man's apprehension to even coming in contact with *Shocking Terrors* #13 was convincing even a skeptic like myself.

"And I assume the buyer got his hands on it?"

"Oh, yes, the man went to the dealer's home and found him in a terrible state. He was decrepit and sickly, and delirious. The buyer offered him one thousand dollars for the book and it was said he was very glad to be rid of it."

He got real serious, "Even though the old man was delirious, he grabbed the buyer by the arm and warned him not to ever read its pages.

"And the buyer, did he read it? What did he—"

"Now, the next bit is somewhat disturbing," he cut me off, "it is said, the buyer couldn't wait to return to his hotel room with his newfound prize, he went outside to his car and held the book in his hands before opening the clear Mylar snug that kept it protected."

"The cover what did the cover---"

"He pulled the book out of the clear plastic coffin it had been in for decades and opened its pages. Of course he went straight for Fitzgerald Moore's story. And he read it."

"How do you know all this, what happened to the—"

"The man was one of my buyers, I sold to him for years. His name was Roger Alten. He called me that night from a pay phone to tell me this story. I have known Roger for over twenty years and I've never heard him so distraught. It was as if something about his demeanor had completely changed. He tried to tell me the story I just told you, but it was in fractured and disarranged sentences. His pace was frantic as he tried to tell me what the story was about, but as he got to describing it, his words became mumbled and completely unclear. It was as if the story itself was not letting anyone tell it. It only wanted to be read on the page."

Curious, I thought, more speculation into the possession of the manuscript. Chilling, for sure, but I had to believe this was all coincidence. Maybe Roger Alten had suffered from a mental disorder for years and it just then had decided to make its way to the forefront of his brain. Maybe he contracted something from the dealer, his illness, or a bacterium, that had affected him. For sure it had to be that and not the aftermath of reading words on a page.

"Roger tried to get the words out, but he seemed to be getting more and more frightened as he spoke. Of what I had no idea. I tried to get him to tell me where he was staying in Detroit, but he didn't seem like he was able to answer."

"Do he ever make it home? What happened to the book?" I was eager now to know the details.

"It was days later that I found out what happened," His disposition changed, "I got a call that Roger had been found dead."

"Murder?" I asked.

"No one knows. Apparently, at some point in the night, he went back to the man's house he bought the book from, broke inside and bludgeoned him to death with a hammer. The police said they found his brains splattered all over the room and could barely identify him on the count of his head was a pile of blood and mush."

"And Roger?"

"He was also dead, it turns out, he tried to bash in his own brains with the same hammer. And after cracking his skull, and not expiring, Roger roamed the house looking for some other method to commit suicide with. They found a trail of blood and grey matter that travelled the entire house. Finally they found Roger's body in the garage, after finding a bottle of rat poison, he drank it in its entirety and finally, after some suffering and regurgitating his last meal, he expired on the floor."

"And this is all true," it seemed far-fetched.

" I was skeptical too. Roger had never hurt a fly in his entire life. He was a vegetarian. So I asked for the police report, and that's where I got the gruesome details. As insane as it sounds, that's what I surmised from the police and a few newspaper articles I read."

"I does sound bizarre, and I'm sorry for the loss of your friend, but—"

"Listen to me," he got right in my face, "When I say stay away from that book, I mean it!"

"I get it," I said as I got up from my chair behind the table, "again I'm sorry for your loss."

As I got up, I felt a strong hand grasp my arm. I turned to see John, the book dealer, giving me the most intense stare I had ever see.

"Take this," he handed me his card, "If you ever come

across that damned book destroy it. If you feel that it has," he paused, "altered you in any way, give me a call. Do not hesitate, your life may depend on it." He seemed very convincing.

I exited the dealer booth and walked away with an uneasy feeling about me. Not for the insane story he just told me, but for with the intensity that he told it. I was convinced his friend met and unnerving death, but was its cause the book that I seek?

I didn't get a chance to ask him, what happened to the copy of *Shocking Terrors #13*, but being the only known copy I was able to start tracking the provenance to, I am going to hopefully assume that it survived the encounter and somehow found it's way to an antiquarian book or comic dealer in the Detroit area. Even though the incident just described to me was years ago, it was all I had to go on.

I looked at my convention program to see if any of the dealers present were from Detroit or surrounding cites and sure enough, Devon King Used Books was at booth #105. I made a b-line for it immediately.

The booth had a myriad of sci-fi, horror, crime and comics, so that was a good sign. The prices were reasonable and there were a few dollar bins. I started browsing through the pulps to see what the selection was. *Weird Tales, Astonishing Stories, Planet Stories*, he had all the staples.

"Got any new collections?" I asked the man who I thought was Devon.

"Sure, right over there, an estate sale just came in the other day, I have gone through them all yet, but feel free to pick through it. They don't have prices yet, but I'll give you a good deal. Unless you find Amazing Stories #1 in there."

"Ha." I laughed, "I'll be sure to let you know. I dashed for the bin that was the bounty from the estate sale. This could be the one that contained the book I had searched so hard for.

The estate sale loot was in a comic book long box. It contained a bunch of pulps, magazines and comics. I quickly flipped through the comics, and got to all the pulp sized periodicals. *Future Science Fiction, Other Worlds, Terror Stories*, it was much of what I had seen on the other tables, and then I came upon a 1950s issue of *Wonder Fiction*. It was bagged and the cover was loose, but it moved in a way that revealed another cover behind it. I raised it up but not too far out of the box so the dealer could see what I was doing. I opened the clear Mylar bag and got a whiff of the musty newsprint that secreted from every aged rag from this era. I lifted the fragile pulp magazine out and to my surprise, the tattered cover of *Wonder Fiction* fell away to reveal a different title altogether.

A chill came over my body as I looked upon the cover of the book I had sought for so long. It was an old and weathered copy of *Shocking Terrors #13*! I could hardly believe it. My hands started to sweat. My pulse raced as I gazed upon the cover illustration that was on of the most disturbing things I had seen. It depicted a man, who looked like he was in the ninth plane of hell, being overcome by a horde of demons. The look on his face was so horrid and pained I could hardly stare at it for long. The man's eyes pierced mine and I felt a peculiar shock to my brain. The magazine looked authentic, it did not appear to be a bootleg copy. And there was his name and blurb right on the cover; *Inside: A New Horror Tale By Fitzgerald Moore*. I tried to pull it together, yes indeed; I was holding a real copy of *Shocking Terrors #13*!

"Find anything good in there?" my heart skipped a beat as the man I was calling Devon, peered over at me from the other side of the booth.

"Yeah, a few things, I think." I shuddered for a minute, and wondered if 'ole Devon knew of the legend of this rare and ghastly periodical. I quickly put the issue back in the bag and let the cover of *Wonder Fiction* hide what was really in the bag. I grabbed a few other issues, as to not arouse suspicion and went to the register.

"Nice score," Devon said as he looked at my stack of books, F*uture Science Fiction #76,* great issue. *Other Worlds May 1953, not bad, Terror Stories #54…"*

Then he got to the bottom of the pile, a bagged copy of *Wonder Fiction.* My heart was pounding as he peered over it, if he chose to open the bag he would for sure see what was behind the façade.

"You know, Wonder Fiction was on of those rare books that had sci-fi, horror and erotica in its pages."

"Oh, I didn't know that.

"Oh, yeah, he continued as he shook the book in front of my face, "this here's got some really twisted stuff for the time, I mean it ain't the porn crap that you read today, but for the 50s it was pretty risqué."

"That's, uh, good to know, I'll be sure to check it out."

"Yeah, you do that. How about twenty bucks for all of 'em?"

"Deal. I said," I couldn't get out of there fast enough. I handed Devon the twenty-dollar bill said thanks and left.

Holy crap, I was freaking out. Not only did I get the most rare book in the history of pulp horror, but I got it for five bucks! I headed out the door with an excited smirk on my face that I could hardly contain. On the way out I passed by the booth for John's Book Nook, and John was eyeing me like an eagle, with a discerned look on his face. Did he know I had scored my prize? His demeanor shot down my enthusiasm for a second, as I remembered his tale of horror and his warning.

I'll keep it in mind, I thought as I made my way past the incoming crowd and out the door. I felt safe once I was inside my car and locked the door. I dare not take the issue out of its protective bag and behind the veneer of the tattered cover of *Wonder Fiction.* You never knew what crazy fan or dealer was looking over your shoulder, thefts happen at these things all the time, especially when they knew the issue was a rare and valuable find.

I started my car, drove out of the lot and made it out to the open road. Whew. I could not feel more relieved. Now, what to do, I thought. Do I wait and let this settle in for a minute, or do I go for it and read the tale that has been so forbidden it is the story of myth and legend. I had to admit to myself, that in the time I had started looking for *Shocking Terrors* #13, a little over five years now, the lurid tales of dread and horror of what happened to those that have dared to read the books forbidden pages, had been creating in me a slight feeling of panic and aversion.

I wasn't going to let it get to me. I came this far in search of the abandoned piece of fiction and I couldn't not indulge it.

I made it to the motel I was staying at which conveniently located right off the highway. I went inside, put my bounty on the bed and went to the bathroom to freshen up. Upon returning I couldn't keep my eyes off the book, as if it was beckon me to read it. I took it out of the case and removed the false cover of *Wonder Fiction* and laid it out on the bed so I could marvel at it.

Shocking Terrors #13. I was staring at a genuine copy. An original. Albeit, nit a pristine mint copy, as it had been read and handed down for decades now, but it was in very good condition. The spine was tight, the cover has somewhat of a sheen on it, and the pages, while yellowed, weren't that delicate. While the cover image still disturbed me, it was a stunning piece of artwork to observe.

I gently picked up my prize and flipped to the contents page. I saw the editor's name Caleb Johnston. The publication date was published Winter 1953. That checked out with what all of my research had revealed. The list of authors was that of mainly unknown up and coming talent that I had heard of, but I'm sure the names would not be recognizable to anyone outside of the hardcore sci-fi and horror pulp genres.

There was a tale entitled "Dreamer's Horror" by Alonzo Hamilton, "The Spirits of the Lake" by Sigmond Gruber and "The Book of the Dead" by Irwin Drake among others. Scrolling down I found the one I was so desperately searching for; "The Chameleon" by Fitzgerald Moore. The Chameleon. In all the time I had been looking for the reclusive story I had never even come across its title. It was good, a little creepy, but not something completely horrific that I would be compelled to read it on title alone. Moore's other two known stories, "The Doom That Came From Space" featured in *Haunted Horrors* #3, May 1946, and "The Strange Case of Ridley Johns", published in Terror Tales #9, August 1947, had much more of a horror feel to them for sure.

Strange that Fitzgerald's last Published horror tales was August 1947 and he didn't have another published until Winter 1953, which was the ill-fated *Shocking Terrors* #13. I was curious about the long delay.

I slowly flipped through the mag and took in the 1950s typefaces as I whiffed the stale musty newsprint. The illustrations were also a bit crude, as they seemed to be rendered by newbie illustrators, but they did have a disturbing and morbid feel to them none-the-less.

I got to page thirty-six and there it was, the title page to "The Chameleon" by Fitzgerald Moore. There was, of course, a black and white pen and ink illustration to go with the story and it was of a disturbed and contorted man of about thirty years old, that was looking over his shoulder to spy a small winged demonic imp sitting on his shoulder.

I read the first words…*Twilight had come upon the slopes of the vineyards…*

As I progressed through the tale I could see at the outset that it had all the staples of a Fitzgerald Moore tale. Run on sentences, descriptive horrific words, experimental structure, and bizarre typefaces. And while reading, Moore kept you glued to the pages, building the suspense with every paragraph, while the chills went up your spine. As I read the words I could feel the images he described burning their way into my mind unlike any story ever had before, I experienced a throbbing pain unlike a bad migraine that seemed to keep pounding as I read. My pulse began to race as if I was being chased by some unknown thing that wanted to get me. It was similar to the fears one experiences when waking from a terrible nightmare.

I began to feel a strange weight pressing down on me as I flipped through the pages. When I began to read the tale I devoured the words with reckless abandon, but around the midpoint I began to hesitate as I got to every page turn. It was as if there could be some heinous twist to the tale that would actually affect my mental state, already going afoul. Moore's words were now becoming illegible and resembled passages from some occult book similar to *The Deamonolie Necrocans* or the *Bibliotheca Resurrection*. The words were not of any language I had ever known and soon, it seemed like some unknown force had taken control of my vocal chords and I was reciting the passages over and over again, aloud in the room. I could hear myself saying what seemed like occult sonnets and haikus, but I could not stop myself. I could hear scratching sounds coming from the walls, or was it behind me, or even just in my head? I could not tell. My throat became dry and parched, but I continued on with what now seemed like chanting. My head pounded as I felt fingernails or claws scraping at my back, the pain became more intense, but still I could not put the book down.

Again and again I repeated the words on the page, not even recognizing what I was reading, I could not even decipher what I was saying, the sounds emanating from my larynx were of a resonance and tone that was equally disturbing as it was ear piercing. My body began to quiver and convulse as I could barely turn the pages, but my hands were like a vice grip on the bedeviled tome and I could not for the life of me put it down.

I began to see things in the air that I knew were not there, but they were crystal clear. Screaming mocking faces and horrific eyes and winged things were projecting at me and seemed to be ethereal-like but then pass through my skin. They didn't seem to go through me, but found a home inside my body, like I was a vessel that was waiting to accept them. Each time my body seemed to swallow on of these berserk fiends, I felt my own form become more bloated and distended.

As I turned the to the last page, my body was shaking and convulsing like I had been administered an amphetamine and hallucinogenic drug that had gone very bad.

Finally I reached the end of the cursed tale and like magic spell the entire frenzied experience came to an abrupt stop. I threw the book on the bed and attempted to make sense of what had just happened. My body was writhing in pain, my head throbbed and my arms had scrapes and cut on them that were not there before. I had always stated emphatically that I was a skeptic of all things paranormal, but now I was wishing I had heeded the warnings of all those who had told me not to seek out this haunted book.

I went to the sink and splashed water on my face. I stuck my head under the faucet and swallowed as much water as I could to relieve my sore and hoarse throat.

I wiped my face and looked at myself in the mirror, my eyes were dilated, my skin had broken out and I had a rash that travelled down my neck and onto my chest. It began to itch like a bad case of poison ivy and I could only scratch it with a frenetic pace that seemed to make it worse.

I took the terrifying issue of *Shocking Terrors* #13 in my hands. I camouflaged its face with the ripped cover of *Wonder Fiction,* placed it back in the bag and then inserted that into the plastic sack the dealer had given me so it was out my damn sight.

I paced around the room and wished I had a Valium and aspirin to relive the ills that seemed to have invaded my body. I had an extreme weight on my shoulders that seemed to be a malevolent presence. I could only think of the bizarre illustration that accompanied Fitzgerald Moore's bewitch tale, of a man with a blackened demonic imp sitting on his shoulder. Is this what I had been possessed by? It seemed insane, ridiculous, yet I know the terrifying visions and strange inflictions to my body were real.

Paranoid, I began looking out the window, to see if anyone was outside my room. Surely someone had heard the ruckus I had created and was wondering what type of a madman was lurking behind my door. The parking lot was near empty. There were only a few cars and no one seemed to be around. I was safe for now, but for how long?

I needed to phone someone? A friend? To tell them what had happened? What would they think? They would commit me. Should I call 911? Would they think I was on drugs? Would they lock me in a cell, so I couldn't hurt myself? Maybe that was the safest place for me. I had to call someone that would be sympathetic to my plight. The dealer, who warned me, John, he gave me his card.

I fumbled through my pants pocket and pulled out a crumpled business card for John's Antiquarian Bookstore. I went to the motel phone and hastily dialed the number.

"Hello?" I heard the voice on the other end.

I tried to speak but, "Meghfgnndhegh," was the only thing that cam out of my mouth.

"Hello?"

"Maggaflabbb-llgbgb-gbgngbg," again I mumbled through and incomprehensible series of words and phrases.

"Who is this?" the voice on the other end sternly asked.

"Mmgagag-hagafrg-flrgbb-gbb-glbb, " I tried as hard as I could to explain myself, but nothing coherent was to come out of my mouth.

"It's you isn't it? The man searching for the book. You found it didn't you?"

"Llgbgb Maggaflabbb-Fggb-gbgngbg," I wanted to explain myself, I needed help.

"I warned you but you didn't listen!" he berated me, "where are you?"

"FFllgb-Maggaflabbb-llgbgb-gbgngbg," maybe I was having a stroke I thought.

"You were warned. Destroy that book before someone else has to die!"

I slammed the phone down and realized I was in a very bad predicament. The rash on my neck and chest had spread to my stomach and groin and I could do nothing but scratch at it until the blisters bled. My head was pounding so hard I could not make it stop. I began pounding my head against the wall. *Make it stop! Make it stop!* My brain pleaded with the unstoppable force that was delivering my misery.

My head seemed to crack, as the blood splattered against the wall. I wondered if I had slammed my head so hard I had fractured my skull.

BANG! BANG! BANG! I heard a ferocious knock at the door.

"What is going on in there?" I heard the motel desk clerk yell, "You're disturbing the other guests, I'm going to call the police!"

"Mmgagag-hagafrg-flrgbb-glbb, " I yelled back at him, but nothing but stammered nonsense came out of me.

"What are you on drugs? You Goddamn addicts! I can never get rid of you!" he screamed at the top of his lungs.

I paced around the room; I had to get out of here! I tried to pack up my things. I was in no condition to drive, but maybe out on the open road I could clear my head. Before I could get to the door I heard a key go into the lock from the outside.

"I'm coming in you druggie bastards!" I heard the man on the outside say.

As he tried to come into my room, I could only grab him, I needed to make sense of what was happening to me.

"FFllgb-Magflb-llggb-gbgbg," I screamed as I struggled to tell him I was possessed.

"I've had enough of you addicts," he grabbed me by the neck and started chocking me. As if some superhuman force had taken control of me, I flipped him over and threw him to the ground. He struggled to gain the upper hand but I proceeded to pummel his head with my fists. Again and again I beat him until my knuckles were raw and bloodied and his face was a sanguine mess of flesh and bone. I stood up, now covered in blood and looking like a maniacal madman, the flashing red and blue lights quickly enveloped my room, as did the sound of a police siren.

"Come out with your hands up!" I heard the words I had listened to on so many cop shows now directed at me. From the bed, I grabbed the copy of *Shocking Terrors* #13; I had to tell them it wasn't me who did this. It was this accursed magazine.

I stepped forward to the doorway, covered in blood and bodily fluids, my head was cracked open and I was sure there was grey matter oozing out, I held up the bloodied magazine in one hand and tried to explain my terrible situation.

"FFllgb-Magflb-llggb-gbgbg," I screamed I heard a cacophony of gunshots go off. I could barely register the sounds as I felt hot metal pierce my body one after another. I stumbled back, still grasping the ill-fated newsprint book in my hand as my head smashed against the cold hard worn carpet of the motel room floor.

I could see myself spitting up blood as the two officers entered the room with their guns drawn. I could feel my life fluids exiting my body as I went cold.

I tried to raise the book to show the officers, I had to explain to them, what had happened, I had to warn them of the dangers.

An officer grabbed the plastic shielded pulp magazine from my twisted hand. He looked it perplexed, as it was smeared with blood and you could barely make out the ripped title of *Wonder Fiction* now deteriorating with the cover of *Shocking Terrors* #13 peeking through.

"FFlgb-Magb-llgb-gbbg," I mumbled as he looked over the object that was now evidence in a murder/shooting and then looked at me.

How could I tell him he needed to burn it, get rid of it so it never hurt anyone ever again? I choked on the coagulating fluids that were erupting from my esophagus. I watched as he placed the book into another clear bag, an evidence bag that would keep and protect it for years to come. Maybe it would be safe, preserved in plastic and shielded from society in a police evidence room

It would be safeguarded from prying eyes, that is, until someone like me, a sleuth looking for a lost piece of bedoomed fiction came calling. I guess it would be all right, all right for now. I felt the last bits of my beating heart get weaker and weaker as I awaited the blackness to come.

End.

DEAD THING

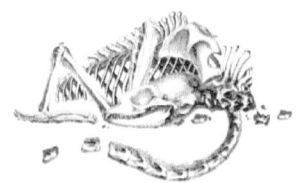

Many a solitary afternoon had I spent wandering the woods alone. I would spend many a lonely afternoon walking in the woods alone. I passed my time and thus, I cleared my thoughts. There was always some excitement whether or not I'd see some rare bird or contorted tree stump. On most days there was something new to discover on the other side of the street in those dense and far-flung woods that still lingered there from a time before the houses came. But never, in all those solitary wanderings, had I come across something that troubled and disturbed me, not until the ill-fated day I stumbled upon *the dead thing*.

I t was an overcast afternoon, the day I decided to take a stroll into the dark wood. I grabbed my trusty walking stick, my backpack, a fishing knife and a few sundries in case I ran into any trouble. I always carried a small first-aid kit, and being a boy of only twelve, this impressed my parents---so many children would wander into the forest without a second thought. Being a few years into my Boy Scout membership I knew the motto well, *Be Prepared!*

And prepared I was, for any challenge or confrontation that might have come my way or flown into my face. Ready as I always was, nothing could have prepared me for what I would find that day. My trusty backpack carried a water bottle, compass, first-aid kit, an extra jacket, flashlight, matches, dry socks and a walkie-talkie. You never know when another person with a walkie might be near you; hopefully scanning channels, and come across your cries for help. Ha! I laughed at myself. Cries for help? I'd been in these woods many a time and the worst thing I ever came out with was a sprained ankle and a bad case of poison ivy. Nevertheless, it paid to be prepped.

The entrance to the woodland was clear. It had a sign that read *Willow Hole Trail.* It was an old sign, created when sign painting was an art form. It had that gold leaf trim that was fading from years of weather and winters, but it still spoke of a time when more care was taken in crafting signs.

I scampered down the hill and followed the trail, still wide enough for two people and well trodden. Not a root or stone was in sight to trip my way. I jumped over *Sneak- Stream*, took my chances on the *Quail Wall*, an old rock wall rumored to have been built by the early settlers of New England, and finally came to *Garret's Fork.*

The trail split here, and knew if I went left, or south, it would take me to *Adam's Pond.* Some great adventure would wait me there for sure. There were plenty of bullfrogs and small turtles to catch and let go, as well as salamanders and sunfish to marvel at. But I had been there many times, and I was feeling that I needed something new, something to challenge my curious boy mind. I had taken the right path, or north fork as they called it, a few times, but only made it about fifty yards before turning back. The trail got a bit harrowing and it always seemed to be getting dark before I worked up the nerve to traipse down its greatly revered and hollowed narrows.

But today was different, it was high noon and I had just put a fresh set of batteries into my flashlight, and even though it was overcast, I knew the daylight would last at least five more hours.

Off I went into the unknown, determined to find adventure. Soon, I came upon *Barker's Log*, a giant tree that had fallen across the path. It was too big to be removed, and over time, had rotted and was now the home of untold amounts of creepy crawly insects. With a good head start I gathered enough momentum to easily hurdle the timber and avoid being overcome eaten alive by flesh-eating centipedes!

Now I was getting to the point on the *North Fork* trail that I had never been down. It was marked in my mind by a giant moss-covered rock. The massive boulder resembled some type of tortured animal, with a writhing head, twisted body and malformed legs. Covering the entire surface, a rich green moss resembled a strange dense fur. My parents had recently got a subscription to HBO and neglected to apply any parental controls, so late at night I would stay up, and with the volume down, watch untold hours of R-rated horror movies. My parents always warned me not to watch them as they'd give me nightmares, and they were right! The darkness of my closet was now infested with hiding demons that wanted to lunge out and eat my soul. Even in our family yard, clouds and trees now appeared as horrific monstrosities and lumbering ghouls. Only the illumination of the sun's rays would ease my troubled over-imaginative mind. This was the reason that a two-ton granite mass of twisted stone now resembled some mutated life form.

But on I went. Excitement and enlightenment awaited me in

the deep dark woods. As I plunged further into the towering timber wilds, I noticed the trees and undergrowth had taken on peculiar characteristics. The tall straight growths that I had passed by only moments before were now replaced with curved and hunched-over thickets and thorned shrubbery.

The trail was getting narrower as I travelled deeper into the coppice, and the canopy above me seemed to clasp closed like gnarled fingers. The time clearly said it was 1pm, but it seemed closer to dusk as the thick branches blocked out what little sunlight there was.

Coming over a small hill I inhaled a rancid smell that burned my nose and caused me to hold my breath for a moment. I took a few steps more and then—then--I *stepped on it*. I heard a disgusting squish that turned into a crunch as my foot trod into something vile.

I looked down to see a wet mass of discolored hair that was covered in scurrying insects. Stepping back in revulsion, I realized this horrid stench was coming from the coiled mass below me. A mangled leg and vague claw shapes told me this was a carcass—a carcass of *something*!

A decaying rodent? A rotting opossum? Maybe a dead, diseased raccoon? It didn't look like any animal I could recognize, and at that moment I had christened it *The Dead Thing!*

I stepped back and wiped the bottom of my shoe against the moss and roughness of the wood. The stench and the grotesque image froze my heart, and a deathly sweat trickled down my back. As if mesmerized, I could not tear my eyes from the lifeless mass at my feet. With one hand I held my nose, and with the other I moved my trusty stick in its direction. I poked and prodded at its hair, or what might be fur and realized it felt quite firm in some areas and pliable in others. I had always assumed anything dead would be soft and mushy, because of the rot. I was experiencing the many stages of decay and rigor mortis first hand.

A recent rain matted down the creature's fur and I tried to find the location of its head. The tail was easy to find as it jutted out the backside, but was crooked and I could see bone peering through the decomposing flesh. My stick had a sharp point at the end of it, as I had used my Swiss Army Knife to give it a nice point right before my hike. I was able to prod at the immobile thing with ease, but I could not find its head. It was the size of a raccoon, maybe a little bigger, but its color resembled an opossum. It was gray with a little white, but its tail was black, where an opossum's was usually pink. I could see something like a leg sticking out with claws that looked more like the talons of a walking bird.

I sweated more now, drawing bugs and mosquitoes. Another precaution I took was to bring insect repellent. I sprayed myself with this oil-based yellowy aerosol and hoped it was enough to keep blood-sucking pests at a safe distance.

I had a nagging desire to see what was inside this varmint carcass that was lying at my feet. I crouched down to get a closer look. My stick navigated its way through the matted hair as I tried to find a face to this mysterious thing that had peaked my curiosity. I found what may have been its head at one point, but it had been decayed so much that I could not contend that the bone was skull or otherwise. It had been shattered as if some blunt object had smashed it to bits. Was I looking upon a ghastly murder, I thought? Did some psychopathic abuser of animals, who would crush this small creature for none other than the sport of it, do this terrible deed? I had to wonder. There was evidence of this type of thing that would creep up now and again in the press. A local dog or cat would be found dead, and got there by dubious means. Or was this small creature just the victim of the forest food chain. Maybe survival of the fittest reared its ugly head once again and I was just the witness to its outcome.

Again, I doubted this, as the carcass was not eaten. There were no bites, no chew marks and no sign of a scuffle. The only creatures interested in feasting on this thing were the lowly insects, which would pretty much eat anything.

I tried to lift up my little friend and see what was underneath it. A stretching sucking sound echoed through the woods as I peeled the remains from the moist forest floor. More vermin scampered away as I tried to discern what this decrepit thing was.

I still could not find a head per say, only a mangled ball of flesh and bone that had some type of a socket that was home to a bulbous blackened sphere. I gazed into the darkness and tried to discern what this poor creature had endured in its last moments. A myriad or horrid deaths raced through my mind, but if a predator was not the cause, then what?

Disease. It finally occurred to me that these woodland critters could be the victim of a terrible sickness just as humans succumb to cancer and respiratory illnesses, why couldn't a similar culprit be lurking in the dark wood?

I adjusted my bandana as to be sure not to inhale any bacterium or spores, although I'm sure it was too late at this point.

My inquisitiveness was burning. I had to figure out the cause of this thing's passing. I flipped its body over and revealed what I thought was its belly. It was pinkish in color and had what looked like six nipples on the underside. Ah, I thought, it was female. Now I was getting somewhere. Could its nest or litter be somewhere close? Crying out for their mother? Surely any new born reliant on its parent, would be deceased by now.

I used my pointed stick to puncture the soft under-hide. The thing emitted a poof-like sound, as its innards seemed to be filled with gas. I laughed at the noise, reminding my of some Saturday morning cartoon impact effect, but I was quickly repulsed by the noxious vapor that filled the air. Before I could retreat, an expulsion of guts and slime shot out of the globoid form and covered my hand and arm.

GOOD GOD! I thought, *it got on me!* The horrid contamination was on my skin. I dropped my stick and reached for anything in my backpack to wipe myself clean; my first aid kit, a towel, some anti-bacterial spray? I had my water bottle, which was half empty, but was enough to wash some of the gore off my arm. I used a rag I had also packed to wipe the rest off, but the dark sanguine color only seemed to stain my skin, much like the spray-on tan you see advertised in the drug store.

I was disgusted, what was this contagion that was now seeping its way under my flesh. I had to get it off. Curse you! I screamed at the dead thing before me. I grabbed my pointed stick and proceeded to stab at it again and again as if to kill it over and over. I was merely curious and now this thing had accosted me with its poison. I stabbed and stabbed until all of its insides were seeping out.

"Take that! You bastard!" I screamed as I jammed at the decaying carcass with all my might!

I ran as fast as I could back the way I came to the stream I had crossed hours before, maybe I could wash it off there. I ran and ran, never looking back. I had forgotten the time and only now was noticing the darkness that was creeping in over the forest canopy at an alarming rate. My flashlight! It was in my backpack, which I had left behind in my hasty retreat. I only had my trusty walking stick that was now covered in the plague that had infected my arm. What was I doing still holding it in my hand? I tossed it as far as I could into the trees and brush and continued on forward, trying to make my way to the cleansing water that could be my salvation.

I began to sweat and my breathing was choppy as fear overtook me. I learned in the Boy Scouts that panic could be your undoing in a situation like this, but that was no comfort. My psyche was completely taken over by dread and anxiety and there was nothing I could do to stop it.

I soon came by the stream I sought and proceeded to bathe my entire arm in its flow. I scrubbed until my skin was red; to be sure to eliminate any trace of the toxoid substance that I was sure had infected me.

Once I was positive the ghastly venom was cleansed from my hand and arm, I tried to breathe a sigh of relief. I dare not look back as I thought I'd see some *thing*, some *creature* following me out of the terrible and fearsome wood. I looked forward and kept a steady pace until I was clear of the timber jungle and onto the street where I finally had some contact with civilization.

Over the next few weeks I watched my hand and arm closely for any sign of contagion, and to my horror a pinkish rash had started to spread where the gory slime had attacked me.

Soon the rash had turned into lesions that leaked a green puss, it was so disgusting that I dared not show anyone or I'd be thrown into a quarantine or given some untested vaccine or worse. I wrapped up my arm with a bandage that had to be changed daily and only wore long sleeved shirts that covered my hand when the cuff button was left undone.

Soon the infection had spread to my upper arm and chest and was giving me nightly discomfort where only sleeping pills would allow me the escape of slumber.

I did not know where this would end up. I had taken some left over antibiotics I had from tooth infection a few months ago, but to no avail. My malady was only getting worse.

After many years and many doctor visits, the infection didn't seem to improve. Various doses of antibiotics, both in pill form and intravenously, only gave me temporary relief of symptoms. In the years that followed, both my parents would inherit infections similar to mine. A small rash would appear that would soon grow and spread over the entire body. With my parents advanced age, their immune systems were not able to withstand the ailment, and they both expired within a few years of each other. Realizing my infection was contagious I became a recluse and barely left the confines of the house that was left to me upon my parents death.

I was able to make a modest income by writing for various blogs and newspapers that needed articles on anything from sports to obituaries.

It is now years later, and I sit alone, friendless and frightened, an agoraphobic who can barely set foot outside for fear of spreading my terrible syndrome, or acquiring a new one.

Once in a while I get the courage to peer out of my curtain covered windows, seeing the outside and its frolicking inhabitants, if they only knew the horrors that could befell them at any moment. Would they be so careless to walk among the edges of the woods, or near a vacant lot of tall grass?

Thinking only of my predicament that I was sure was going to lead to my demise; I could only express my regret for taking that unknown path into the darkest of woods that day. Where there are stranger and stranger creatures, some living and some dead, neither stone nor flesh, waiting for an ignorant passer-by to be the victim of its lust. I have never gone back and only sometimes wonder what my parents think happened to their little boy—as I only told them I had gotten a poison-ivy like rash from a strange bush I grazed when I went on that fateful hike. I had never told them about my encounter with that thing in the woods that was dead.

Over the past few months, my affliction has appeared to become resistant to any drugs either antibiotic or antiviral. The rash and hives now cover my entire body and I ache from the inside out. Any mirrors in my house have been cracked as I can barely stand to look at myself. A pale comparison to my former human self, I've transformed into something more decidedly animal than homo sapien. I've come to accept my new form, even with its hideous characteristics and putrid smell; I've decided that it's convenient and favorable to my current situation.

I have never copulated with a woman, as one could guess, I haven't had much contact with anyone but my parents and a few doctors that came by the house in full protective gear. I thought parthenogenesis was just something lower animals or insects experienced, but as I saw my abdomen increase in size over the last nine months I could only surmise that I was to give birth. And sure enough, within a few days of when I would have considered myself full term I gave birth to a half dozen small mammal like crawlers. After which my form developed breasts from which the suckling's feed. I can only guess that this new form I had become, had realized it was nearing the end of its life-cycle and with no host to jump to, it decided, all on its own, to propagate itself. Being alone most of my life, and having to care for no one but myself, I now had purpose.

As I lope and crawl and writhe, my lips drawn back from

my new fangs, my wonderful new body with its matted fur and closures of claws, if only my parents knew how happy I am...in the wonderland into which I was led by *THE DEAD THING.*

INCIDENT AT THE
HAXFORD INN

The cart creaked with each revolution of the wheel as the light rain tapped at the tarp protecting me overhead. The driver and horse remained unbothered by the chilling weather, but I had to pull my coat tighter to myself as I tried to read the paper in my hand. Adjusting my eyes to my shaking hands, I continued to read about the missing boy.

His name was Cameron Howard. He was fourteen years old and last seen by his friends going into Haxford Inn. A group had searched the entire vacant estate but found no signs of the boy. They searched the town of New Canaan, Connecticut and surrounding areas for multiple days without any leads. He hadn't been the first missing person that encountered this ghostly inn and I intended to get behind it. America needed a story that would get them interested in something other than post-civil-war life and I, the up-and-coming reporter Julian Van de Vosse, was going to bring it to them.

The cart lurched to a stop and I handed the driver a few cents, "keep the change," I said as I stepped out into the sprinkle. Before me rose a three-story building with two large Romanesque towers on either side of the main entrance. One of the windows in the tower appeared shattered, but when I rubbed the rainwater from my eye, I could see that it was solid. I waved to the driver as the cart began to leave me behind, but I got no such fancies in return.

I jogged up the long path to get under the protection of the pavilion over the patio. Being a supposedly closed establishment, I was surprised to hear voices coming from the downstairs lobby. I nearly entered the inn, but I could hear music playing from the other side of the doors, so I knocked instead. Not long after, one of the two doors swung inward and the pale face of a man in his seventies peered back at me. He tried to smile, but it came off as a discomforting smirk. It must've been him making music, as it no longer drifted in the air. I looked inside and saw no one. The voices had stopped, but I was sure of what I had heard only moments ago.

"Hello, welcome to the Haxford," the man said and gestured for me to step into the building. I hesitated a moment, but then entered the dim-lit room. "Will you be staying with us for the evening?"

"I thought that this place was long abandoned?" I asked.

"Oh dear, another one of you folk," the innkeeper said as he went behind a desk and grabbed one of the room keys. Half of the keys were gone from their places. "People spread the rumor that this ol' place is nothing but a dust mill, but that's just a childhood rumor. Two dollars a night."

"That's a little steep," I said as I fished for my money in my pocket. "So, you never saw that boy that went missing?"

"I'm afraid that's another story that got blown up by the headlines," the innkeeper said and gestured towards a stairway nearby. "Your room number is twenty-two."

"I'd like to speak with you about the disappearance, if that's alright."

"Oh, sure," he responded, "like I said, it's all a misunderstanding, that boy is a local prankster, who has been perpetrating untold mischief around here ever since he realized he could."

I nodded and thanked the man, then made my way up the stairs. I listened intently for discussions between people in their rooms, but I couldn't hear anything except the faint tapping of rain echoing throughout the building. When I reached the room, I entered and locked the door behind me, then checked my pistol in my waist to ensure that it was still ready in case I needed to use it. It was loaded, six bullets and a hair trigger. It came in handy when fighting the Confederates and it gave me a true sense of security.

I hadn't expected there to be anyone in the hotel, so my plans to search the inn would have to wait. I took out my notepad and scribbled a few notes, before falling asleep. When I shook myself awake, it was still raining, but the small window in my room revealed it was the night at last.

Placing my gun back on my waist, I peeked out of the room carefully and listened for the innkeeper or anyone else. Not even so much as a creak came from the old house. A few of the doors were ajar, so I glanced in to find that the rooms were completely empty even of furniture. A glance down the stairs revealed that the innkeeper no longer waited for visitors and the room was swallowed in darkness. I cautiously took the steps down, so I wouldn't wake anyone and because it only got darker as I descended.

In the main entryway, I waited for a moment and listened for anyone or anything. A sound came from a closed door. It had to be a boiler room as it sounded like metal groaning under the expanse of heat, but when I opened the door, it sounded more like a backed animal growling. I waited for the sound to stop then checked over my shoulders for the innkeeper once more; nowhere in sight.

Each step felt as if it would give under my weight, but I pressed on. A small light came from the room at the base of the stairs, I knew it had to be the boiler room, but I was shocked when I found a room filled with tables that might have once been a cellar. A single candle flickered in the middle of the room and a box resided beside it. Was the Innkeeper nearby? I glanced around and saw no one.

I stepped over to the box and candle with care while checking below each table. What had caused the noise? After realizing that I was the only one in the room, I moved over to check the small wooden coffer. I held the candle so that I could see inside the box, which I opened slowly. Besides dust and a smell of mildew, a bunch of photographs resided in the bottom of the box.

The first few were only pictures of people inside of the inn, a few guests, a family, a newlywed couple, but as I shuffled through them, others appeared stranger. The photos were old, and their color was of a sepia tone, but a few had accents of color, as if they were hand tinted. Some of the people in the photos wore dark robes with their faces covered. I stopped on one of the pictures, which showed the very room that I stood in, but without the tables. In the center, one of the robed individuals drew circles into the ground. I peered down and noticed the remnants of scribblings below my feet. Curious. As I flipped through the distorted pictures, I observed that the figures were in contorted poses, almost painful to look at. And many of the faces were blurred, as if they were in motion and the old camera that tried to capture the moment, could not maintain a steady hand to focus. One showed a man screaming; I could make out the pained look on his face. He wore a tormented look that I had never seen before. On the battlefields I saw many a man suffering from bullet or knife wounds, but nothing resembled this. Another photo showed a woman, tied and bound to a post; she was blindfolded and had cuts and bruises all over her body. There was a short pudgy man in the background, his face displaying a demonic smirk. I nearly vomited at the next photo when it revealed the same bound woman having her neck cut with a knife. As horrified as I was, I continued onto the next.

The succeeding photo showed the woman's body on the floor with a strange creature standing over it. Obscure as it was, I could still make out the strange form. The creature appeared to be a darkened shadow with the form of a tall thin man with curling bat wings. It was shocking to see color in the photo, as the creature's eyes were red against the black and white. I peered into its sanguine eyes for a moment before noticing that the monster moved within the photograph.

I dropped the photo and the guttural moan that came from the dark corner of the room caused me to leap and drop the candle. Just before the light extinguished with the flame, I caught the outline of the same ghastly figure that had been in the photograph. Had it never left or did it jump right out of the photo? I didn't wait around to learn more of it as I spun and darted for the stairs.

In my haste I stumbled and fell over one of the tables, I could hear the thing's breathing as it wandered toward me. It sounded like someone fighting the worst case of pneumonia mixed with the garglings of a salivating beast. Even through my fear and urgency for the stairs, I could smell the putrid odor of rot clinging about it. I felt for the stairs in the dark and could see them just a bit from the small amount of illumination trailing down.

I used all four to propel myself up the stairs, but just as I reached the top step, a moist hand wrapped around my ankle and yanked me back down. My body slammed against each step until I kicked with my free leg. The beast stopped pulling me then gave a loud snake-like hiss and I felt multiple teeth rip into my calf. I kicked once more and the hand released me.

At the top of the stairs, I slammed the door shut and stood with my back against it for some time. Nothing tried to force its way through and I couldn't hear anything on the other side. I glanced at the front door and nearly took a step towards it when I heard someone walking nearby. Above me, I noticed a small balcony around the main room and the innkeeper stared down at me.

"The door is locked, m'boy," the innkeeper said. "It's best if you stay here."

"Help me!" I shouted there's a thing in the basement"

"A *thing*?" he mocked me.

"I've been bit, my leg its—" Glancing down I saw there were no bite marks on my leg.

"You were saying?"

"I swear, I felt it, a creature attacked me, it was---"

"Your imagination is running wild. You're tired from your long trip."

"You did have something to do with the missing boy?" I said. "I saw the pictures."

Before letting him answer, I darted for the front door. As I reached for the handle, the door swung open of its own accord and slammed into me. The oaken monstrosity quickly slammed shut as I fell to my hands and knees. My head, now throbbing, was projecting a harsh ringing sound, which echoed through my skull. Behind me, the creature lurked out of the basement. It stepped towards me until I pulled the pistol from my waist then blasted a hole through it. It screeched as loud as a high-speed train grinding on the brakes and I ran.

Up the stairs and towards the end of the hall where I'd noticed a window earlier in the day. I sprinted for the window then dove through it. The glass shattered and fell to the ground with me. After hitting the hard earth, I spun and looked up at the broken window where the innkeeper looked down at me with a contemptuous smile. I ran from the inn as fast as I could and didn't stop running until my legs burned even in the cold rain. When I thought I'd made enough distance from the inn, I dropped to my knees to take a rest. It had all been true, the missing boy and anyone else that had entered that foul place; they just hadn't made it out alive. When anyone went there to search in big groups, the building must've been abandoned.

I had to get the story out, I couldn't let anyone else end up there whether it be a kid on a dare or homeless that seeks shelter from the weather. When I glanced down to again check the bite mark on my leg, there was nothing. No scratches. No bite marks. I still could not believe I was unharmed. I continued to hear deep rasping even after I'd caught my breath. Something followed me and lurked in the trees along the roadside. I stood then started at a fair pace, whatever was following me would have to come out of the trees to get to me. I held fast to my revolver.

The snapping branches and deep grunts forced me to a run even though my legs threatened to give underneath me. I noticed distant light ahead of me, which seemed to be someone with a lantern and an umbrella. I waved for them to turn around, then started to shout when the person didn't respond.

"You have to get away from here, there's a--," I stopped in my tracks and swallowed the rest of my words as the man came into focus. It was the mad innkeeper. He stood before me with a toothy smile. The rain trickling down the umbrella made an ungodly sound.

"I believe you're quite right," he said. "We do need to get away from here."

The bullet that I fired into the man's gut ran red, but he remained with perfect posture and an unyielding smile. He made no attempts to stop me as I ran past him, but when I glanced over my shoulder, he still meandered towards me. My body only ran on energy fed to me through fear.

I reached the town a few miles through the forest. The rain soaked me to the bones and it felt as if the sun would never return to the sky.

As I entered the small town, I passed by a tavern with people drinking and smoking out on its patio. I had to tell somebody, so I started to approach until I noticed one of the men sitting in the group was again, the innkeeper. He was unharmed and eyeing me as if I were carrying the plague. Thinking I may be suffering from exhaustion and mild hallucinations, I kept my distance. I needed rest and I needed it soon. I walked down the street, now fully soaked, looking for another inn to stay the night. Luckily I found one a few blocks down. I breathed a sigh of relief when I noticed the innkeeper at the front desk of this inn, was a different man. I needed to sleep. I needed to rest my weary head and body until the sunlight washed away the ills of this terrible night.

"Is it almost sunrise?" I asked the new innkeeper after purchasing a room.

He gave me an unusual glance then said, "The midnight bell tolled not long ago."

I found my room and ensured that the door was locked behind me. There was a window in the room which I jammed a candleholder against so it couldn't be opened, then covered it with the curtains. I sat on the edge of the bed trying to comprehend what had happened, but my head swam with thoughts. At first light, I'd grab the watch and take them back to the inn where I could show them the room. I cursed myself for not keeping the photographs, even though they held horrific images, they were my only proof that something foul was at hand. This inn at Haxford was truly cursed.

I contemplated sleep, but my racing thoughts only led me to lay on a bed in the darkness. I'm not sure how much time turned until the smell crept into the room, rotten and foul. Leaping from the bed, I checked all the corners, but couldn't see the source of the smell. A tap came from the window, which froze me to the spot I stood on. I thought standing silently in the darkness would be enough to make the room seem vacant, but the tapping persisted. When I pulled the curtain aside, nothing resided on the other side.

I let out a sigh of relief, and then turned back to the bed. Emerging from the darkness, a shadow figure reached out for me. It was the same winged demon that has accosted me back at the bedeviled Inn. I dove for the door, hurried out, and slammed it behind me. One of the other room doors lurched open and the maniacal innkeeper of the Haxford stuck his face out to grimace at me. I kicked the door shut in his face, then ran for the entrance of the inn. The Haxford innkeeper stood before the entrance, so I took out my pistol and fired. The shot hit him right in the chest.

As the innkeeper's body slumped to the ground in a red voice, his voice came from behind me, "What do you think you're doing?" I spun on my heels and there he stood again in the hallway. I fired again, spraying his blood against the wall, but when I turned for the door. There he stood again, standing over his own body lumped on the floor.

"What the hell is going on?" I asked as I raised my shaking pistol to him. "What are you?"

"Once you've entered," The innkeeper said while taking a step closer to me, "you don't get to leave."

"Stay away from me," I said and squeezed the trigger. The innkeeper fell upon himself in a heap.

A hand grasped my shoulder and I spun, firing my last shot into the belly of the one holding me. My heart stopped as I realized it was not another incarnation of the Innkeeper, but an old woman who'd touched me on the shoulder. She clutched at her bleeding gut, then dropped to the floor. I glanced about the room, only lit by candlelight, and took in the sight of the people lying on the floor. None of them was the Haxford innkeeper. I glanced at their tormented faces, who were these people that I had just shot? Am I a murderer? I was sure I had fired at the Innkeeper, or some apparition version of him, but, no, it seemed I had shot a half dozen people I had never seen before.

I shuttered and collapsed to my knees and the front door burst open. Several men with rifles came streaming into the inn and circled me with barrels pointed towards my skull. The men glanced around at the scene and me, and then another reached over and pulled the gun from my hand.

"What on God's green earth happened here?" a man

wearing a golden star asked as he entered the building.

"The Haxford inn," I said. "It's haunted."

"That ol' building has been gone for years," the sheriff said and he clapped irons around my wrists. "Burnt down in 1875 after some lunatic claimed the same thing."

"But I was just there," I said, " I swear to you I was!"

"You imagined it, probably intoxicated on bad absinthe or tainted whiskey."

"No!" I insisted, "I haven't had a drop I—"

Just then flashes of recent events flooded my mind. The man I thought was the Innkeeper, standing in the road, with the umbrella, was a man, reaching out to me, trying to help me. And I shot him. The other people, at the Inn, also appeared as people trying to assist me, and I shot them too, believing they were the insane innkeeper.

I shivered as I was led out past the dead bodies and out the front door. A horse-drawn cart waited for me.

"Save it," he said as he pushed me up into the cart, then took a seat across from me.

I lowered my head as the cart lurched forward, ashamed that my mind had gotten the best of me. It must've been in my head the entire time and something was wrong with me. The cart moved for a long time, so long that I finally looked up from my hands and out the front of the cart.

A flash of lightning revealed the Haxford inn just at the end of the road and its innkeeper who drove the horse towards it. I turned to the one sitting across from me and met the red gazing eyes of the creature enshrouded in the shadows. In his clutches was a young boy of about fourteen. It was Cameron, the boy who went missing, the boy I came to find. He looked frightened, he reached out to me, he was calling, needed my help.

"Cameron," I shouted through the bars in the window of my wheeled prison, "I came to help you!"

I turned to the front of the cart and banged on the wood separating me from the driver, my metal shackles digging into my wrists and drawing blood, "Stop the cart! There's a boy out there, he needs our help, he been taken by a dem—" I stopped myself. *A demon?* Is that what I was going to say? The driver didn't respond. Nor did I want him to. I came to my senses. Was I really thinking that a demon had taken a boy hostage and was going to take his soul to the netherworld? This all had been a delusion. The inn, the innkeeper, the demon…it was all a lie. I had killed six people thinking they were ghouls or ghosts. I was the one who needed help.

I crept back to the back of the cart and peered out of the window. I could still see the winged demon standing in the middle of the road as the rain poured down. I watched the boy reach his hand out to me and was about to cry out before the devil's bat-like appendages opened up and wrapped around the boy clutching him like so many spiny fingers. The shadow then moved straight backward in an inhumanly movement as if it were floating on the air, and disappeared into the darkness.

I turned around and lowered my soaked head, and looked at my battered body. What have I done? I would be tried and convicted of murder. I would surely be hanged. And for what? To chase a story of a missing boy in a haunted town in New England? I had surely gone mad, and now I would pay for it.

I would spend the next few years writing down my story and trying to convince people of the circumstances that happened at that bewitched rooming house. No one ever believed me except a few editors that wanted to turn my tale into a Penny Dreadful, a new type of printed story that was gaining in popularity among the masses. I took them up on it, as it paid me a royalty, which I used on lawyers to try and appeal my   case.

It was all for naught, as I awaited my hanging day, I kept playing over and over again in my head the occurrences that be felled me on that fateful night. Was it real or not? I could barely tell now as the memories where just as blurred and faded as the pictures that started this whole horrid journey. The journey that took me to the incident that occurred at the Haxford Inn.

THE INSIDIOUS DOOM

I. The Whispering Town

The windshield wipers creased back and forth against the rain-splattered glass as Davian Cooper drove along the snaking road. The car shuddered a moment causing the headlights to flicker then shut off completely. Then it rolled and halted in the middle of the road. The twisting of the key gave no new life to the vehicle, so Davian stepped out into the storm and glanced the car from bumper to tailgate with disappointment.

He knew that his destination only resided a couple more miles ahead, so after gathering a few belongings from the car, Davian headed for the town of Thurmond. He was glad to find a flashlight in the glove compartment alongside his pack of smokes.

It was difficult to enjoy smoking when the rain drove

towards him and the forest on either side of the road creaked and moaned with each gust of wind. Davian thought nothing of the trees and their shadows until one appeared in the center of the road as if someone stood before him. After searching the area to no result, he pressed on through the bitter cold.

The town's sign appeared in the light stream, then he noticed the first abandoned building— a small house with peeled paint, shattered windows, and a collapsed roof. It was neglected, but the building next to it seemed promising. He knew that one of the few towns' residents was an inn operator who lived right near the entrance. Firelight flickered through the dirt-stained windows and a small trail of smoke rose from one of the building's two brick chimneys.

Davian wrapped his hand against the door and a slow pair of footsteps echoed from inside. The door swung open to an elderly man who hunched over his pooch. One eye was pale with cataracts while the other was so dark it appeared that he only had black in his iris. Without a change of expression, he motioned for Davian to step in and out of the rain.

The warmth from the hearth enveloped him as he removed his coat and placed it on a coat hanger. He followed the old innkeeper as they entered a large sitting room with several couches around the fire and a small bar in the corner.

"Care for a drink, young man?" he asked. "I don't have so much as a full bar, but I have a few delicacies."

Davian took the seat closest to the fire. "I'll take bourbon if you've got any," said Davian.

"Ah, a man with similar tastes," he said as he took a bottle off the top shelf. "So, what brings you to Thurmond?"

"Well, I'm a paranormal investigator," Davian said as he took the hi-ball glass from the man who sat across from him sipping his drink. "There's been quite a few claims now of strange happenings around this abandoned town."

"Mostly abandoned," the man said. "A few others and I still live here. We like the seclusion nor want to leave our memories behind. I'll tell you though, a few people have come poking around these parts looking for the same thing you're searching for and most of them haven't liked the results that they've found."

"I'm sure that I'll find something of worth to bring back," Davian said. "Whether it's proof of spiritual activity or proof that there isn't anything."

The man smiled as he swallowed the last bourbon from his tall glass. "So, I take it you'll need a room for the night?"

"Yes, and may I use your phone to call a repairman for my car?" Davian asked.

"There are no phones here," he said. "They never saw it fit to bring 'em here. Just be careful where you go poking around. This ol' town is falling apart. Some buildings are more dangerous than others. My name is Miller Newman."

"Davian and thanks for the warning."

"You know, I've heard all of those tales as each of those people carrying the stories have stayed here," Miller said. "I don't believe any of the non-sense, I've been here almost every day of my life and not seen a lick of it myself."

"Do any of the stories have anything in common?" Davian asked. "A certain location or event that happens?"

"The rail station seems to get a lot of attention from you visitors," Miller explained. "They say you can hear the train's horn blaring as if coming into the station, but the damn tracks haven't been live for years. Apparently, there is a lot of whispering around there too. I'm telling you though; it's a waste of your time. I'm turnin' in for the night."

"Thank you for letting me stay here," Davian said.

Miller nodded then pointed to a bedroom door as wandered towards the stairway. Davian thought to put the fire out, but its embers crackled low, so he assumed it okay. The room was quaint, and a thin layer of dust clung to everything, so he slid down the window to let in the fresh air. His walk up to Thurmond helped force him to sleep, but he woke only a few hours later before the sun rose. Rain still smattered the roof.

As he tried to force himself back to sleep, a soft voice entered through the window.

"If I don't catch the train, I'll never make it out of here."

Davian pondered on whether he'd only begun to sleep into a dream, but then he remembered what Miller told him of the train station, so he urged himself to throw the covers off and quietly exit the inn.

The road of the town bore spider web cracks throughout making the town appear as if it had been struck by a large earthquake. The collapsed buildings revealed that it was all a testament of time. "Hurry, it's about to leave." The whisper forced Davian to spin on his heels, but no one stood near him. No woman to be the owner of the voice.

After walking a few blocks, Davian glanced around realizing that he should've asked the innkeeper for directions to the train station, but then he noticed a nearly illegible sign, which said "Depot" on it. He glance at his watch showed that it was three in the morning, but he knew that couldn't be right as the clouds were growing a little lighter.

As the train station came into view, a train horn blared as if a train were leaving from the station, so Davian ran to the depot. Nothing resided inside and the tracks even appeared to be separated in several locations. It had been years since a train passed through the station. Water dripped through the cracks in the ceiling and the walls had growing vines that attempted to break into the structure.

The horn blasted once more, but it was echoing from far off in the mountainside now. Davian considered following the tracks but knew that would be a pointless endeavor.

"Now, we'll never get away from him."

Davian searched about for the whisper, but only he resided inside. The place surely evoked spiritual energy, but how had the innkeeper resided here so long without experiencing it? After searching the train depot further to only find piles of rust, Davian wandered back out into the streets unbothered by the incessant rain.

"Is anyone there?" Davian shouted then peered down each path that led to the train station.

A crackle caused him to tense. He looked over to see an old woman who'd kicked a tin can as she shuffled towards him. She held an umbrella, but it had a few tears and appeared to be older than Davian.

"What's all of that shouting about?" she asked, inching closer to Davian.

"Sorry, were you inside the train station just now?" he asked after glancing at the station over his shoulder.

"In there?" she asked and pointed at the crumbling building. Davian nodded. "I don't go in there, only fools go in there. Best not to be a fool. Abandon this city like the rest of them."

"Why do you stay?" Davian asked as the woman turned and

meandered away. She spoke nothing further which pushed him into considering her one of the spirits inhabiting the town. He thought to follow her but decided it best to leave the woman alone on her walk.

He spent the rest of the morning searching through a few buildings while poking his head into dark rooms. Many of the inhabitants' belongings had been left behind and now items were rusted or rotted in their fixed place. A thick film of black mold coated most of the walls and covered the once colorful expression of human life.

When Davian returned to the inn, he couldn't find Miller, so he set to making the fire himself. It was only the beginning of fall, but the long and icy fingernails of winter clung to the town and tainted the rain. He spent a few hours writing notes in his small notebook before Miller returned. The old man stopped in the doorway and stared at him as if he were a stranger.

"I didn't think you'd stay another night after seeing the rust bucket here," Miller said.

"Some interesting things happened while I was exploring," Davian said as Miller poured them each a glass of bourbon. "I heard whispers, they told me to go to the train station and then I heard the train."

"That can't be. The train hasn't operated in years and those tracks are in ruins," Miller said. "However, you aren't the first to make claims about hearing whispers. Last few visitors mentioned something about whispers, but I think y'all are just hearing the wind as it bends with the river."

"I met an old woman too," Davian said. "She carried a bad umbrella."

"Ms. Copperfield," Miller said. "She was the beauty of the town back in the day. Poor lass refuses to leave and she's more stubborn than I believe she and I are the last ones here unless that one couple still lives on the stretch of property in the corner of the county. Did I tell you the story about the demon they say lurks the streets on moonless nights?"

II. The Street Lurker

"You could have said something about that last night?" Davian asked as he finished his bourbon.

"I'm telling you they're just stories," Miller said. "I would've seen a creature as tall as the buildings walkabout on one of the many moonless nights I've lived here. Are you a religious man?"

"Not particularly,' Davian said, "but I do believe that there are malevolent energies in the world, and this might be one of the sites for it. If I can find any proof of this demon, then you might have more devout people than I arrive at your doorstep."

"That's the last thing that I want," Miller said. "A traveler from time to time is nice, but a flock of them would make my head spin. I can't be sure where the moon has been as it's been raining for days. I don't recommend searching the grounds at night. If you're hurt, no one will be able to rescue you."

Davian nodded then retreated to his bedroom. He waited until the light faded from the other side then set out into the streets. Though the rain slowed, the weather was on the verge of freezing. With his flashlight, he found the signs, which lead him to the main street where he rested on the only intact bench.

"Run faster or it's going to catch us," said the voice of a boy darting behind him along with the splashing of rain puddles. It was if several people ran by, but he saw no one.

He ran in the direction of the voice in time to hear it from around a building corner, "Don't let it see us." Davian searched all directions, but no form of a pursuer came into sight. His flashlight caught the shadow of a child darting down an alleyway, so he followed and found a steep hillside.

"Go faster, it's coming," the boy's voice came from the top of the hill and several handfuls of rocks slid down. Davian climbed up the muddy hillside until he reached the flat. It took him a moment, but he noticed the entrance to a mine a few paces away.

At the entrance, he shined the light in and at the far end he saw the shadow of three children, but no bodies to cast them. The gravel separated beneath his foot as he took his first step in; his light never leaving the shadows. Several tentacle-like shadows reached into the light and wrapped around the children.

"No!" Davian shouted.

Children's screams filled the cavern followed by the snapping of hundreds of bones. Davian froze with his light fixed on the back of the tunnel. The shadows are gone. A loud gurgling came from the tunnel then loud snaps when sent Davian out of the tunnel. He slid down the hillside, then waited for a moment; waited for some strange creature to come barreling down the hill for him. Nothing followed.

Davian glanced up at the iron-grey and black clouds. Had the moon saved him? Taking the time to let his heart slow, he scanned the area with his light. He'd been to houses where strange occurrences happened and asylums with self-slamming doors, but he'd never experienced anything to the level, which Thurmond proved. He cursed himself for not having his camera with him and considered marching back to the car to retrieve it. He hadn't expected so much as to hear anything, let alone see something, which could be photographed.

Starting to follow the main street, he made his way towards the inn, but only made it a few steps when he heard clicking from inside one of the buildings. In a dark corner, he flicked the switch on his light and held his breath as something slithered out of the building nearby. On the ground, a tentacle slid around the corner as if feeling like a blind man, then hastily pulled away.

No sound indicated that the creature left, so Davian resided as motionless as possible. An hour passed and he began to shake from the cold, which drove him to peek around the corner. Nothing stood in wait, so he darted from his spot like a mouse in a restaurant and ran for the inn in the darkness.

When he got inside, he closed himself in his room where he secured the door and the window. He tried to sleep in the bed, but his eyes remained fixed on the window until the clouded sky seemed to change to a greenish hue.

III. Forgotten Dreams

Davian tried blinking, to clear his eyes, to see if the green tint was caused by overexertion but it remained. At the window, he peered out to see the town in full life. The buildings were no longer crumbling and falling while people walked the streets waving to one another. Stepping out of his room, Davian looked around for Miller, but couldn't see him among the people sitting in the gathering room. They all seemed real, dressed in clothing that was forty years out of fashion, and when his shoulder met another man's shoulder, the man glared at him. He stepped outside and the swirling green clouds like a slow hurricane drew his attention to the sky.

Three small boys ran past him, but one of them stared at Davian the entire time. They all seemed so familiar. The townsfolk spoke to one another in a friendly manner and none of them noticed the churning sky above. Davian felt for the pulse in his neck as he began to think he'd slipped into death. His heart still raced.

"Hey, what's going on?" Davian asked a man holding a newspaper. He pointed up, but the man looked past him as if he weren't even there. When Davian reached up to tap the man on the shoulder, his hand breezed through the man leaving him untouched. "Can anyone hear me?"

"I can," Davian turned to see a woman about his age. "What do you need help with, dear?"

"What's happening?" Davian asked.

"Come with me," the woman said and took Davian's hand into her own.

She led him through the people on the streets and weaved through the alleys until she reached a large road that they followed to a large white church. Before they approached the church, she pointed up and Davian could see through the swirling clouds that it was night and the moon nowhere to be seen. When he returned his gaze to the earth, the woman stood near the church peeking slightly in the corner of a window.

He reached her side while crouching, then joined in spectating. A man in a black robe stood in the center of the church where all the benches had been pushed aside in disarray. A body lay on the floor at his feet and he held a red dripping knife in his hand, Davian stood as if to break through the window, but the woman motioned for him to duck back down.

"It's too late," she said. In the distance, a train horn sounded. "We have to go, or he'll feed us to it too."

"Feed us to what?" Davian asked as the horn echoed out

once more.

"Hurry, the train's about to leave."

The woman sprung from the spot and darted in the direction of the depot. Davian checked inside the church one last time to meet the hooded man's shadow enshrouded face staring at him just from the other side. The church floorboards creaked as the robed man started walking for the door. Davian didn't wait any longer and chased after the woman who was nearly out of sight racing through the town.

All the people that had been walking the town were gone except the young woman, him, and the hooded man who walked after them. A screeching howl came from the church making Davian and the woman run faster. When the train station came into view, the horn blasted again as the train moved away from the platform.

Davian grabbed the woman's hand and urged her to run faster, but it was too late. When they reached the station, the train already rounded the bend in the track. The woman made for the tracks as if to chase the train, but the impact of the train wreck caused the ground to tremble. Smoke rose into the air from the crash site followed by the same howling they'd heard from the church.

"Now, we'll never get away from him," the woman said.

She collapsed to her knees as trees splintered nearby. Davian tried to help her back up, but she stuck to the ground like a heavy stone. Tentacles reached out from behind a building, extending towards them. Davian urged the woman to move, but she remained fixed, so he turned and dashed away just as two tentacles wrapped around her like a starving python. The creature never came out from behind the building as it ripped the woman from her spot. The sound of her scream was the force that drove Davian to wake.

IV. The Picture of Evil

Davian opened his eyes to the window and the iron-grey clouds growing lighter with the morning sun. Sweat clung to his skin and his heart pounded; he felt as if he hadn't slept in days. He checked out the window to find the ruined town still abandoned. When he left the room, he found Miller waiting for him in the living room with a cup of coffee. Davian chugged down the coffee then asked for another.

"Decided to go out at night?" Miller asked.

"I saw it," Davian said. "The demon or something of the sort."

"I shouldn't have told you any of those stories," Miller said. "They've gotten to your head."

"Miller, you can't stay here," Davian said. "This place is evil. I had a dream about it and I saw the people that used to live, what happened."

"I'm not leaving," Miller said. "This is my home. You're starting to sound like all the other cucks that come around here search for ghosts. I think you're all mental. I presume you'll be off now?"

"I'm not crazy, this place is wrong," Davian said. "I'm going to go back to my car and retrieve my camera if I can get a picture of what I saw last night, then my story will be believed unlike everyone else."

"Do what you must, young man," Miller said, "but don't let it get to your head even though I think it already has. It'd be better for you to spend your time walking to the next town to get help with your car."

The woods around the town felt drearier than they had the previous days. Davian continued to search the trees for anything reaching out towards him. He debated about taking Miller's advice but decided on staying.

Crackling from the forest startled Davian as a young man stepped out of the woods. His clothes were dirty and soaked from the rain. They stared at one another before the young man stepped out onto the road. "Don't see strangers around these parts too often," he said. "Ya leavin' town?"

"Actually, I'm just heading to my car to get something," Davian said. "It died further down the road."

"If ya come by my place later, I can help ya get it fixed," he said. "My wife won't be too happy, but nothin' ya can do there. Now, I've gotta find my chicken flock that's runoff, but the sooner yer outta here, the better."

"Why's that?" Davian asked.

"Damn town's cursed," he said.

"You've actually seen things?" Davian asked.

"This town is evil," he said. "My place is on the bend of the river."

Before Davian could ask the hundreds of questions boiling up in his head, the young man darted off in search of his livestock. Davian only felt the urge to leave the town for a moment, but when he reached his car, his will only strengthened to stay and get proof.

When Davian returned to the town, he passed the inn and took a few photos of the area. With as much information as he could collect on his few nights in Thurmond, he decided it best to write a long piece to send to academic journals and would need photos to go alongside it. His last paper had been deemed unworthy of the intellectual community and dismissed as conspiracy, but he knew this was too good to miss.

Miller sat on the porch of the inn with a pipe where he rocked back and forth. He observed the paranormal investigator with a mocking smile even as he joined on the porch and lit one of his smokes.

"You're just like the others," Miller said.

"We are the others, paranormal investigators, as well?" Davian asked.

"I don't believe so," he said after blowing one smoke ring through another. "But you all expect to go back and have people believe you. What do you think? They'll just flock here and give you fame for discovering an abandoned place?"

"It'll give credibility to my field," Davian said. "People might start taking these things seriously rather than chalking it up to mental hysteria or fictional stories."

"No matter what you take back, they'll still label it for what it is," Miller said.

"Come with me tonight," Davian said. "You can see for yourself."

"That'll make a believer out of me," Miller said. "Let's have some grub."

The night fell with the heavier rain, but Miller had an umbrella for each of them even though they whipped about in the fierce wind. They made for the church in the town where Miller claimed the last traveler saw the demon. Davian hoped that the whispers could be heard, but only the wind through the buildings muttered.

At the church, Davian checked the window before entering with Miller following behind him. The benches were still pushed to the sides, just as he'd seen them in his dream. His flashlight revealed nothing inside, and Miller began to grow impatient.

"You know, I haven't been inside this church since the day my father died," Miller said. "You happy you found a dust-filled mess?"

"I just figured there'd be more," Davian said. "My dream was so vivid."

Davian pulled his hand back after running it along one of the benches. A sharp edge had sliced into his finger and the blood trickled down to the floor. A clicking came from the dark corner of the ceiling. Davian's light fell upon it holding itself up in the corner. A thing with an octopus-like body with a head resembling a mantis with mandibles the size of Davian's arm was somehow holding itself to the crumbling plaster. Davian could see that it was the creature's drooling mouth and teeth, moving back and forth, causing the maddening clicking noise that seemed to be getting louder. Too terrified to move, Davian watched as hairy and clawed hands dangled down between the tentacles, which held the creature up. The three-fingered spiny extremities wrapped themselves around Davian's neck.

Davian gasped for air as he struggled to free himself from the deadly clutch. He watched as what looked like an elongated slug curled up in the thing's mouth, coiling back like a snake ready to strike.

One of the monstrosity's free tentacles swatted the flashlight from Davian's hand. Now, with two fists flying, Davian was able to free himself from asphyxiation and the sharp claws it had had on him. He quickly dove for the floor, but not for a weapon. Davian grabbed for his camera and he rose up in time to take a photo before being thrown to the ground by a half dozen slime-covered tentacles. The creature dropped to the floor with a sickly thud. Davian, now at eye-level with the hideous beast, realized if he didn't get out of there soon, he was to be devoured, bones, guts and all. Hastily, Davian picked up his camera and the flashlight. He rose and darted for the door, but Miller slammed into his face.

"Miller, what're you doing?" he asked. "We need to get out of here."

"You're just like the others," Miller said. "They all have said that. I'm sorry that you won't be able to return and tell your story, but I'll make sure that it gets out there."

Davian observed the man standing before the door for a moment. He realized he had seen his stature somewhere before. Then it hit him, "You're the one who wore the robe?"

Miller smiled as a tentacle wrapped around Davian's leg and pulled him off balance. Davian kicked with his free leg until another tentacle constricted around him and began dragging him across the floor. The mandibles clicked together as Davian attempted to pull himself in the other direction. The creature's strength overcame him and lifted him into the air.

He stared into the piercing red eyes of the creature that was pulling him closer. The thing's mouth opened wide, the slug-like snake tongue recoiled and this time struck Davian dead in the mouth. He could do nothing as the slimy serpent-like appendage slithered its way down Davian's throat. He tried to breathe, but was unable to inhale even the tiniest breath. He felt pains in his abdomen as he envisioned the mandible-like choppers beginning to eat him from the inside out. The creature began to devour Davian, with its tentacles excreting a foul bile that seemed to digest him before he was consumed. Strong tentacles began to crush his body and the snapping sounds it caused always seemed to make Miller uneasy. The drooling slime, the flapping feelers and the spiny finger-like things, those didn't seem to bother him.

With a smile, Miller picked the camera up from the floor. Photographs of creepy buildings were always allowed, but any evidence of infernal beasts was surely not. Miller opened the camera and exposed the film to what light was left. He watched as the beast slithered across the floor and lapped up any blood or bodily remains of Davian's corpse. Miller gave the tentacle monstrosity a quick stroke on what passed for its head before shooing it off into the darkness. He thought of what was in the cupboard as a long day like this would always call for a hearty meal before bed.

The town began to see more visitors as pictures and tales of Thurmond spread. The rooms at Miller's inn were always open.

THE STRANGE TERROR
FROM BEYOND

CHAPTER ONE

I woke up long before dawn today. I was roused from bed by a dream that sent waves of shock across my entire being. It was unlike any nightmare I have ever had before; it was a chilling and disturbing vision of what was to come. I saw my friend and colleague, Crawford

Tillinghast, in the dream. He was in a terrible situation as a monstrous beast was trying to swallow him whole. I could only see him from the top of his head to his waist. The lower half of his body was in the mouth of the creature that was slowly devouring his body inch by agonizing inch.

The entire scene looked like it was neither on Earth nor any plane of existence meant for humanity to dwell. It appeared like a different realm, a realm where levitation was possible, where the ground vibrated and constantly emitted thick clouds of smoke, where the sky was not white, blue, or dark, but a certain deep shade of green. I had been shocked to the marrows to see my friend struggling in the mouth of the beast. He screamed and writhed but couldn't free himself from the fiend's vice-like jaws. I knew I had to help him, but I could see I was no match for the thing that held my friend captive. Even if I wanted to, in my dream state I was unable to move forward or back. I was paralyzed with fear...or...something ghastly. Tillinghast did not see me at first, but when he did, after moments of futile struggling to escape the clutches of the horrid abomination, he reached out to me for help.

"Lucian!" He screamed with every ounce of desperation he could muster. "Lucian, get me out of here! Help me!"

He stretched his hands in my direction, maybe hoping I would step forward, grab his hands, and pull him out. I could not do that. I tried, but I was rooted to the spot by a force I could not comprehend. I suppose it is the way of dreams to leave you static and frozen at times when you are needed the most. I could not move a limb; I could only watch as the beast ground his powerful teeth into the lower body region of my friend Tillinghast.

As I stared at my colleague tussling for freedom from the fierce grip of the monster, I felt a hand on my shoulder. I was filled with unspeakable dread. I spun quickly to see who had touched me and I was confronted with the sight of Tillinghast standing right before me. I turned behind me and with the utmost confusion saw that the beast, with Tillinghast in its mouth, had vanished.

The newly freed Tillinghast began to whisper words that I could not decipher. The language was that of some alien and profane tongue, one that I had not heard before nor ever wished to. Its syllables and sounds were that of a low growl as if something were scratching at his throat. His face seemed to become whiter with each passing second. A streak of blood flowed down from beneath his hair, down his forehead until it pooled at the tip of his nose and began to drip. Blood was rhythmically dripping to the ground while Tillinghast continued to whisper. I could see he was frustrated that I could not understand him. His face contorted with anger and he began to yell at me, but it made the sounds even more unfamiliar and cryptic. Soon, a black ooze began to slither out of his mouth as he continued to shout at me. The disgusting slime was now being splattered all over me as Tillinghast shrieked and bellowed his maniacal arcane phrases. I was horrified by this sight and the viscous liquid that poured over me. I wished I could just get out of there, but every bit of motion had deserted me.

Tillinghast balled his right hand into a fist for a few seconds, then he raised it to the level of my face so that I could stare directly into his now open palm without having to move my head.

There were a few words scribbled on the surface of his palm in red ink: *Get me out of here. I know you can do it.* The fright of seeing those two sentences brought me back to the waking world.

Presently, I was now leaning against the wall of my room; still disturbed by the gross things I had seen in dreamland. I was not a man to take dreams so seriously because I believe they are manufactured by our brain to add zest to our period of sleep, but this was quite a bit different. I had not been thinking about my friend before going to bed so that I would dream about such horrid things. It was true, however, that I had missed him since his disappearance. I missed even the deeply scientific and philosophical ways of thinking he expressed himself, the very things I did not admire about him when he was still around. Yet, I was certain that my mind had not been occupied with the thoughts of Tillinghast when I went to sleep. How then could it be that I dreamt about him in a manner so lucid that it felt like the images of that dream were still crystal clear in my head while I was awake?

***

"Must be a message from the other side," I mumbled. I went to the window of the room and I parted the silk curtain. I stared into the dark sky. The morning was still far away. The moon and the tiny stars that had ruled the sky just hours ago were now out of sight. I rubbed my balding scalp as I wondered what was next for me to do.

The more I thought about the dream, the more it became clearer that it was a message from Tillinghast. The words that were written on his palm still burned in my mind.

Does Tillinghast know that I have rebuilt his machine? That must be it. I saw no other explanation for the strange dreams. It must be that Tillinghast was alive in whatever dimension the machine had taken him to and now he wanted me to get him back here. Maybe he was in danger. And if the dream was some window into an alternate reality that Tillinghast was existing in, I had to find a way to release him. Certainly, he was in danger. If the beast that was trying to swallow Tillinghast was even a metaphor for what he was experiencing, I had to do all I could to try and get to him.

I heaved a sigh as I thought of what must be done. I had to use The Quantum Generator to get Tillinghast back to this realm. I was not sure exactly how to get him because from experience there were so many possibilities, so many realms to access when one switched on the machine. How was I to know where exactly to find my friend?

"I have to do this," I whispered to myself as I continued to stare at the dark sky. It was a scary prospect, but I had to do it for the man I called my friend. Tillinghast was a good man. The whole discovery of the possibilities of awakening advanced senses and opening the portals to other realms could have taken a toll on his mind. Maybe it had driven him mad, but that did not change the fact that my friend was a good fellow, and if there was half a chance that he was still alive somewhere in one of the multitude dimensions that he had opened up, then I had to do the noble thing and put in my best effort to bring him back. Whether he was sane or not, that was yet to be seen.

I whispered a silent prayer as I headed out of my room in the direction of the attic where I had kept The Quantum Generator. It had been fairly easy rebuilding the machine because I was a man resourceful with my hands. I had kept all of Tillinghast's notes and blueprints on how to build it, and being a student of industrial mechanics, the process went quite smoothly. The bullet from my revolver had done quite some damage, but within weeks I had been able to fix the broken parts and even make some upgrades that would allow me more control over the quantum dimension gates I was about to open.

I felt a mix of emotions as I approached the attic. On the one hand, I was scared and for good reason. On the other, I was excited; enthusiastic about the prospect of bringing to life a man that had been pronounced dead. It would have been difficult for me to be convinced that Tillinghast had been drawn into another dimension if not that his body had vanished from the morgue. I had not thought much about it when it happened, but with these dreams I knew that there was a big possibility of bringing Tillinghast back to the land of the living and I was ready to try.

In spite of my willingness to help my dear friend, I could not accomplish this task alone. I needed to acquire aid. Perhaps in the form of one of his former house-servants? No! They had become privy to the deep dark truths that surrounded my friend and his machine. I needed someone who was ignorant to the truth, but also knowledgeable about quantum mechanics.

Kaitlyn Davidson was considered a child prodigy when she was young. She skipped two grades and graduated high school early. She was only sixteen when she was given a full scholarship to Miskatonic University to study quantum physics. Three years later she was well on her way to be able to pick her place of employment at any one of the top science and technology companies around the world. Lucky for me, she was always at the University, either in the library or assisting scientists with their experiments.

An interview and a promise to allow her to flex her quantum muscles and work on a top-secret off-campus project, was all that I needed to convince Kaitlyn to assist me.

CHAPTER TWO

Kaitlyn adjusted the interconnection processor and was hard at work fixing errors and irregularities in software controlling the Quantum Generator. She beamed. Her face looked especially beautiful when she smiled. I had forgotten what it was like to have an eager female co-ed working next to me.

Kaitlyn became heavily involved in the rebuilding of the generator because I failed the first time I tried to bring Tillinghast back from the realm beyond. It was the fault of my own in my passionate frenzy. She assured not a thing was incorrectly put into my place as my advanced age made me quite forgetful at times.

***

That early morning after I had woken up from dreaming about Tillinghast, I had gone into the attic, full of hope. When I got into the small room, I switched on The Quantum Generator hoping to find my friend through the brilliant display of countless brightly colored objects, images, and otherworldly creatures that were sure to reveal themselves as the machine powered up.

The moment I turned on the machine, my sense of hearing was besieged by a thousand sounds; sounds that I could not determine their sources or what they meant. It was like the first time and the room seemed to expand. I saw different dazzling rays of light.

I peered into the kaleidoscopic reflections, wondering how on earth Tillinghast had uncovered the secret to something this powerful and what some may consider sacrilegious to the normal order of the world.

It was a struggle to keep my thoughts balanced for long. The swiftly changing projections before me made concentration difficult, if not impossible.

"Tillinghast", I muttered to myself. "I have to get Tillinghast."

As soon as I thought of my friend in specific terms, I began to see flashing images of him in one of the corners of the room. I could see him lying on the floor, writhing and contorting as he let out a pained scream. There seemed to be a beast standing very close to him but one, which I could not see. I had surmised that this must be the beast Tillinghast seemed to be locked in some kind of battle of wills from the dream I had.

"Tillinghast!" I shouted for my friend, desperate to bring him back to this earth as I reached a hand out towards him.

In my ears, my voice sounded like it came from a different source. It was faint, almost drowned out by the hundreds of other sounds that were steadily pounding my ears. Tillinghast seemed to hear me despite all of the cacophonous nonsense around us as he turned to look in my direction. Immediately, he began to run towards me as soon as he made out my form. My heart leaped with joy at the sight of this. I wanted Tillinghast back to life, and it seemed that my wish was finally going to become true.

Tillinghast was approaching quickly, but then something happened, something that made the whole endeavor seem like a failure. As Tillinghast ran towards me, I began to see otherworldly and gelatinous entities that resembled jellyfish to a certain degree, only more demonic in nature. Hundreds of them speeding through the air with great dexterity in their movements, unhindered by any normal limitations once they saw me. They were far behind my friend at first, but it didn't take long before they sped past him. Some of them passed through his body as if he were an ethereal being unable to be pierced by anything tangible. It was horrifying and at the same time fascinating to watch. I knew how dangerous it was to let these things spill into this realm, but I had to see this to the end. Tillinghast seemed as if he were being attacked by the floating, biting creatures that he could not escape. And while they did not appear to make contact with him in particular, their mere presence caused his body to recoil in pain and weaken. Some of those wriggling things swam towards me, straight at the doorway between their realm and ours. They were going to come through and without Tillinghast. As much I did not want to leave my friend in this predicament, I could not allow such monstrosities to enter our world.

I took one last look at Tillinghast and I shook my head, indicating, for now at least, he had to remain where he was. He was shocked then angered. He lifted his hand out to me as if to plead one last time for my help before the squid-like creatures burrowed deeper inside his torso. I assumed he would somehow fight them off and be ready for me the next time I opened the doorway between worlds. I reached for the switch of the machine, and I quickly turned it off.

That next moment everything I had seen disappeared into thin air. The grotesque sounds also stopped for which I was grateful. Two of the monster balls remained after the bright lights disappeared. They rolled in the direction of the machine. Or was it me they came at? I drew my revolver and I fired at the balls. Two quick shots for each ball caused a gush of black slimy liquid to spill out onto the ground. I was relieved to see that the balls were no longer mobile and that I seemed to be still quite the marksman.

I tried to bring back my friend on two more occasions, but I was always thwarted by those swirling balls of chaos. I set about delving deeper into Tillinghast's notes. I discovered that he had constructed the machine in a way that allowed monsters to slip through the realms. There had to be a way the machine could allow humans to be transported through the portals, without the creatures. I knew, however, that making this machine on my own was going to take years. I had to seek the help of someone who had knowledge of the generation and transmission of control signals and quantum gates. That was why I had gone to the engineering faculty of the university— to seek bright minds that could give me what I wanted. I chose Kaitlyn after speaking with at least twenty other students. What's more, the girl used to be a servant at the estate for a short time in order to earn funds for her academic pursuits. I was most grateful she was not among the servants who 'disappeared' as well.

***

Presently, Kaitlyn stood proudly next to the machine, admiring the product of weeks' worth of work that we put in.

"It's pretty, isn't it?" She said, still smiling and beaming brightly as ever.

I wondered if she would still have a smile on her face if she saw the monsters that this machine she helped to create was capable of bringing to the world. I had been careful not to divulge sensitive details to her regarding the reason for making the machine. I kept her in the dark about most of the hideous details. I even kept Tillinghast's note from her. The only detail I revealed to her was that The Quantum Generator would open up the portals to different realms.

"It is quite a beauty," I replied. The Quantum Generator was finally ready. Now, I could save my friend, Tillinghast, from whatever affliction he was facing in the realm that he was in at the moment. "Thank you for helping me bring it to life."

"I should thank you for allowing me to try out something practical after years of being enmeshed in different theories in Quantum physics." She chuckled, wiping the sweat from her brow.

She looked genuinely happy with her work and I was glad that she had been able to help bring Tillinghast's ideas to fruition.

"So, when do we fire it up?" Kaitlyn asked. "You said something about waiting for a few days before using it?"

"Yes," I stated. "I want to call my sponsor to see it first before we start the machine together."

There was a flicker of disappointment on Kaitlyn's face. It was quite clear that she would have loved to test run the machine right there. Who could resist the urge to use something that they have put hours of labor into? I slipped a hand in my hip pocket and brought out the balance of her wage. Kaitlyn's face lit up again as she reached out to collect the money. Oddly enough, earning wealth did not placate the uneasiness many folks feel.

"Thank you," she said.

After some minutes, she packed her books and left my house. I sighed as I walked back to the attic after locking the front door of the house. I got to the attic and braced myself for what was to come. The row of bulbs that surrounded the switch looked pretty inviting as I walked closer to the machine. I hoped I would be able to get Tillinghast out this time. I don't think

I would be able to handle another disappointment in the course of getting my friend back to this realm. More worrisome though, my friend could not survive for long in that demented place.

I hit the switch, causing the engine to roar to life. The first thing I noticed was that there were no loud noises as millions of bright lights began to shine. The images that used to flash during my previous attempts took slower to disappear. Kaitlyn was a genius, I reasoned. She had toned down the extremities that came with Tillinghast's initial design. Now, everything was moderate and stable. I could hear super sensory sounds and see beyond the normal ability of the human eye, but all the things I encountered did not threaten to drive me crazy like in my previous experiences with the machine. This was so much better, no longer did I feel the pull towards the abyss.

Amid the sounds and muttered ramblings, I saw Tillinghast beyond the round frame of one of the hundreds of portals that were opened to men.

"Tillinghast!" I yelled, hoping to get his attention like the other times.

He responded by raising his head. From the distance, I

could see that he was not so eager to come after the disappointments of the previous attempts to free him. Clearly, the failed attempts and the noxious environment around him had mentally and physically crippled him.

"This time is different!" I shouted.

He hesitated for a moment, and then he got to his feet and began to run towards me as usual. I looked around for the balls, hoping that they would not emerge this time. The monster balls remained out of sight until Tillinghast emerged from the portal and collapsed right in front of me.

I knew he had been in a deplorable state before the first incident that claimed his life, yet what I saw now lying in a naked heap right in front of me barely looked like the friend I had struggled so much to bring back. His eyes were sunken and his cheeks flat against his jaws. He looked like a skeleton with a discolored skin crudely stretched over it.

"Thank you," he whispered.

I was too shocked to reply. Tillinghast was nothing but a bag of bones. What on earth happened to him?

I dropped to my knees beside him and laid a hand on his shoulder trying to comfort him. A strange smile appeared on his face as he stared at me. He didn't look like someone who needed to be comforted after all. In spite of his emaciated body, he had a renewed sense of self that dwelt behind his eyes.

"Ah, thank you, my good man," Tillinghast said as he pulled himself upright.

There was a disturbed quality about him now. This was not the Tillinghast that I had known for years. This was a man very different. His demeanor had changed, and there was a strange aura about him that I could not quite place. Tillinghast had become…something else.

CHAPTER THREE

"We need to work on the machine again," Tillinghast announced. "I must make contact with the nether realm once again."

"Perhaps we should wait, I warned him, "There are dangers involved. Creatures who could come through the portal and devour us. Look what happened the first time we—"

"Nonsense!" he interrupted. "I am a unique being now, can't you tell?"

I looked over his body and indeed I could feel a power emanating from him that no mortal should have access to.

"What happened to my weak body of flesh and bones can no longer occur," Tillinghast

Smirked. "I have been granted extraordinary gifts. This shell you call a body can do phenomenal

Things," he said with a slight upward curve in his lips.

I was getting a bit unnerved by this conversation.

It was mere hours after he had emerged from the portal. In that time, he would have been content to remain in the attic and talk about the wondrous beast. It took some convincing on my part before he agreed to take a wash and to have dinner. I thought that maybe cleansing his body would also clear his mind.

Later on, I watched him as he ate and I observed the chicken soup I served him. It was his favorite and I surmised that some comfort food would help his weakened cerebral state.

Tillinghast did not seem to find it at all appetizing. He

confirmed my suspicion when he pushed his bowl aside after one sip.

"Let's go back to the attic," he said. The way he said those words, it sounded like an order, a command that I dared not to refuse.

From the look of things, Tillinghast's mental state, which was already shattered by the events inside the nether realm, had now worsened. It appeared as if he was possessed by an evil that was worse than the devil.

I grew so scared of watching him that I reached for my revolver and held my hands around it just to confirm that it was there. I could not vouch for the behavior of my friend anymore. I had to be on the alert.

After I finished my meal, I had no choice but to oblige to his request to return to the attic. I followed him upstairs and observed him as he took position next to the machine that

Kaitlyn had so carefully constructed to the newer specifications.

"With a little tweak, this machine can do more wonders," Tillinghast said as he ran his hand over the surface of The Quantum Generator.

"More wonders?" I intoned. "Do you want more wonders after the unfortunate event that befell you the last time. I asked Kaitlyn to make improvements to this machine so we can bring you back. Now that you are here I think we should destroy it. If not for ourselves, for the sake of keeping our world pure from those vile creatures."

"I don't see it that way," Tillinghast said. "We can open up a world of possibilities and you are thinking of destroying this beauty? No, Lucian. We have to make something great out of this."

I was willing to participate in the creation of something great, but I was wary that what passed as great to Tillinghast meant something different to me. I had to be vigilant. I knew he was up to something sinister, but exactly what I didn't know.

"Let me show you something," he said.

I kept my gaze on him as he clenched his bony fingers into a tight fist. His eyes rolled in their sockets. I wasn't sure if it was a manipulation of the lighting of the room, but his eyes seemed to change from brown to a fearsome black. He raised his hand up and fire erupted from his fingers. Thick smoke streamed out and billowed towards the ceiling of the attic.

"Stop it!" I yelled. Now, I was genuinely scared of my scientist friend. Whatever happened to him on the other side caused him to possess the power to manipulate the elements. It was mind-blowing and terrifying.

"There's more," he continued. "I can fly; I can change forms. I can do things you can only dream about." I was unsure if he was bragging about his new abilities or simply stating what he was aware of what he was capable of.

I was unsure I wanted to see more of what he could do though. "What great things were you speaking of?" I tried to divert the conversation away from his increasingly disturbing feats of power.

"Oh Lucien, so many," he whispered. "There are infinite possibilities. But we need to make a sacrifice. You should know, my good man, that every good thing in life requires a certain kind of sacrifice."

"You're right," I said. "What kind of sacrifice do you have in mind?" I shuddered to think of what it would entail.

"The ultimate one," Tillinghast said. "The greatest things require the greatest sacrifice.

There is no greater sacrifice than that of the human body."

"You want to kill someone?" I asked in horror.

"Kill? Oh, no my friend. Think of it as a rebirth." He had the look of one consumed with lunacy at this point. "It doesn't have to be death and it won't be by your hands," my friend replied. "You spoke of a certain Kaitlyn, didn't you?" I felt my blood run cold at the mention of her name.

"Don't bring her into this," I pled. "Kaitlyn is not to be involved in whatever dark act that you have in mind." I was unsure if I could even protect her, but I'd be damned if I did not at least attempt to.

"Look at the bigger picture, my friend. Using her will be of a huge benefit to the entire world. Why should we not do it?" He paused and I could tell he was mulling over something. "Ah, I see you are in emotional conflict. Do you love the girl? You look like a man who has a difficult choice. It should not be so difficult to decide. It shouldn't be. . ."

I decided to block out Tillinghast's voice from my head. I was not going to let Kaitlyn fall into the hands of one who was no longer a man in both mind and spirit.

"Where is Kaitlyn?" he asked me. Again the sinister voice was pressuring me.

"I refuse to involve her! Enough of this nonsense!" I shouted, pointing my revolver at him. He rolled his eyes and spread his arms out, beckoning me to shoot him.

"Go on then! Show me your conviction!" Without delay, I fired a bullet aimed for his heart, but as the bullet approached he extended his right arm with inhuman speed and summoned an evil flame to burn it to ash. I put the gun down and looked towards the ground as he cackled. "Perhaps I have been too lenient with you old friend. I shall put it this way for you. Either tell me where I can procure her or...I may just have to pay a visit to your dear family...to ensure your family line ends. Today." I felt my eyes fill up with tears of anger and gritted my teeth.

"She's a student at the university," I replied, finally relenting to his demands.

"Excellent! We must use her as the sacrifice," he declared. "Thank you for the cooperation old friend."

There was a sense of finality about the way he spoke to me. He made it seem that it was inevitable. Kaitlyn had to be sacrificed for the greater good that would lead to the endless possibilities of greatness and innovative things. I didn't think there was anything worth a human's life, so I was careful not to state my view directly to my friend. He looked like he would pounce on me if I contradicted him. Besides, I had tried to assert myself over him but failed miserably. There was a fierceness about him that suggested if I went against his wishes he would no doubt make good on his threats, even though he looked like someone that was going to collapse from insanity anytime soon. I certainly didn't want to go against him, nor any man in possession of profane gifts.

"Okay, I will get her down here," I said to Tillinghast.

"Wonderful," he said. "I will set about reconstructing the machine. It needs to be altered in order for the full effects I have in mind for it to become a reality."

I cursed him silently and made my exit, wanting to run and never to return. But that would only amount to my eventual demise and the demise of my many efforts. So I did as I was instructed to do, albeit with a heavy heart.

CHAPTER FOUR

I kept my gaze on Kaitlyn Davidson as she slowly stirred awake. She looked around, trying to make sense of what she was seeing and feeling. She must have wondered why she had been tied to a vertical table and dressed in S&M bondage gear. Tillinghast seemed to have acquired strange sexual deviancies since he emerged from the realm beyond. He would indulge in peculiar fits of masturbation and seemed to enjoy viewing pornography when he wasn't tinkering with the Quantum Generator. Truly, he had evolved into a perverted man filled with sadistic fantasies that he wished to enact.

I had gone to fetch Kaitlyn, luring her with the prospect of seeing what beautiful realms could be discovered there. I insisted on buying her a drink at the school cafeteria before we came down here. I skillfully slipped a drug into her drink while we were together. Now, she was just recovering from the effects of the blue pills. None of this was done according to my own will of course, nor would I ever think to do it. Yet, I had not a choice in the matter.

"Mr. Holmes, where am I?" she looked around at her predicament, "Please untie me," Kaitlyn demanded the moment she gained control of her senses.

Before I could answer with 'It's not going to happen,' the madman emerged from the shadows.

"You have been chosen for a special task and you have to deliver what is needed," he cackled.

"Let me go!" Kaitlyn yelled. "Let me go right now!"

"You are going nowhere, gentle lady." Tillinghast said. "You are a sacrifice to open the secret doors of the higher realms." More like deeper into realms of more depravity, I thought.

"Mr. Holmes, please let me go." She whimpered, looking up at me with wide eyes filled with fright.

I felt terribly helpless that such evil was going to happen to Kaitlyn and there was almost nothing I could do about the situation.

"I'm sorry, Kaitlyn. I'm really sorry. Please, forgive this man for his sins against you." I could hardly look her in the face.

"I'm not sorry, not in the slightest," the scientist remarked. "I am Crawford Tillinghast and very soon all of mankind will be at my feet. I will bring up some of the greatest innovations man has ever seen. And it will begin today. Everything will start when your blood drips into my vessel." At these terrible words, a sense of justice roused up from within me and I felt myself surge forward at the crazed scientist.

Tillinghast was clearly ready for this and made sure I would not be making the silly move of fighting him. He showed me something that shook me right to the core. He moved his arms above his head and he spun it twice around. In the next moment, he transformed into a big tiger-like monster with dagger-like teeth. His jaw detached from his skull like a snake and his gullet expanded threefold to reveal rows and rows of sharp teeth that extended back into his throat. He stood on his hind legs like a biped and increased his size to over eight feet tall. Unspeakable horror. I could see that he could devour myself and Kaitlyn with but a mere rush of movement. Needless to say, this stalled my feet and I remained frozen in place.

He morphed back into his old self after a few seconds. He

didn't have to say anything. It was obvious that he was affirming his superiority and letting us know we dare not challenge him.

Tillinghast walked to the machine and powered it on. There was a loud roar as different noises began to go off in the attic.

"Now is the time," Tillinghast said laughing.

It was clear that the man was insane. There was no point doubting that for any moment.

He spoke about different things, specifically about Xagdrenuz, an entity he described, as a rare beast that was prepared to pass over to our realm for God only knows what reason.

"I will bring the Xagdrenuz here," he said dreamily. "Yes, I have made a pact with the beast and I am not ready to default." I took a step back instinctively as the name hit my ears.

I had remained silent since I brought Kaitlyn for Tillinghast. The pain was much for me to bear. I could barely stand looking at Kaitlyn as she shrugged on the cross that mad man

Tillinghast was holding her captive.

The modified machine was still spewing out loud noises and forcing me into the dreamlike kind of experience that I had felt the first time Tillinghast and I got in trouble with the original device. I tried to resist, but it was difficult. There were too many supersensory images and sounds to contend with.

From that dreadful portal, a massive shape of hideous proportions lurched forward. Unfamiliar appendages grasped the sides of the portal and forced its massive frame through it. It shrieked from innumerable mouths as it used slimy tentacles to feel about the room wildly. I ducked beneath the table Kaitlyn lay prone on and placed a hand on my revolver.

In the corner of the room, I could see the large beast and marveled at its disgusting features. It had eyes all over. There were upwards of a thousand of them on this beast, and about the same number of mouths and arms of various shapes and sizes. The beast lurked behind one of the doors of the portal, keeping its eyes in the direction where the others and I were.

Out of the corner of my eyes, I could see my friend, Tillinghast, changing form again. I watched as he dropped to the floor and became a large-headed monster with a wide mouth full of dozens of tiny teeth.

He remained on the ground for a few more seconds, and then he gestured to the beast and genuflected as he pointed toward the innocent Kaitlyn. All of Xagdrenuz's ugly mouths opened wide. It prepared to lurch forward to devour the poor girl.

If there was ever a time for a rescue, it was now. I drew my revolver and aimed at the head of the beast. I was about to take a shot when I saw thousands of creatures rolling into this realm. Apparently, Tillinghast had given way for other monsters like him to find their way to the earth.

"Noooo!" I screamed when I noticed that Tillinghast in his new form was preparing to attack as well. I wrapped my finger around the trigger of my revolver, shooting and sending the bullet straight into the head of Tillinghast's new form. Amazingly, the lead bullet connected with his flesh. I surmised that perhaps he could not use both his unique abilities and transformations concurrently. I could thank the stars above for that.

Tillinghast didn't die, however. He merely twisted back to his old form and got back on his feet.

"Your loyalty hasn't always been genuine," he said. "I knew

all along. I'm ashamed that you have decided to abandon greatness because of being on the good books of a wench."

"Shut your mouth!" I growled. "I would have left you in the dead realm, but I saved you because I thought you were of value. Today, I have realized just how terrible the decision was.

I regret bringing you back."

"Your regret has just begun," Tillinghast said as he turned away from me and now started towards Kaitlyn. He wanted to sacrifice the girl himself as the great beast was distracted by our brief altercation.

Tillinghast was halfway to where I stood when something remarkable happened. Xagdrenuz, the monstrous being, jumped at Tillinghast and devoured him by grinding him from the lower half up to the head. Each of the individual arms, mouths, and other foreign appendages bit, tore, chewed, and clawed at Tillinghast's body. He writhed and hollered in pain, as his newfound abilities did not harm the vile beast at all. Bit by bit I watched in abject terror as he was torn to shreds and eaten with the utmost savagery. Once the beast had its fill of torturing him, it opened its enormous and rotund belly, exposing its gigantic fanged innards, and proceeded to suck the mutilated body of Tillinghast into it.

The way Tillinghast perished reminded me of that dream I had in which he was at the mercy of a beast.

The thousands of creatures that had poured into the attic were bouncing around. Some were on two legs; some on four and some had three and some didn't require legs to move. Fearful of what was happening, I raced towards Kaitlyn and I quickly untied her.

"He's become crazy," I tried to explain. "I couldn't refuse him or he would have killed me and my family."

"I understand," Kaitlyn said quickly.

She had barely finished speaking when the Xagdrenuz started towards us. It looked like it had me locked down in its sight. I drew my revolver and started to shoot at the beast, doing my best to incapacitate it. My bullets didn't seem to have any effect on the creature as I heard them bounce off its grimy flesh. There was only one way to put an end to this madness.

"Stop the machine!" I roared, and then I tossed my gun towards Kaitlyn who was already headed for the machine.

Kaitlyn weaved her way through the barrage of creatures that were in the attic. I grabbed an upended piece of wood from the floor and began hacking at the insect-fish hybrid things that were now engulfing the floor. As they came through to our world, they became flesh and blood and seemed to be able to be killed or at least maimed.

Kaitlyn fought her way through until she got to the cursed machine and pumped shots into it. It began to vibrate and smoke. Electro-shocks reverberated throughout the attic and

The Quantum Generator started to malfunction.

Tillinghast screamed that his work had been ruined and that he did not wish to die so soon before achieving greatness. I watched as he clawed his hands deep into the wooden floor, trying desperately not to be consumed by the monster he had made a pact with. We locked eyes with one another and he pleaded with me to save him as he did so in my dream. Only now, I chose not to help him; not anymore. He then cursed my name as the teeth-filled gullet of that horrendous monster consumed him entirely.

Turning back to the machine, I saw that it fizzled and sputtered wildly as the creatures around it began to fade in and out of this plane of existence. I cheered, as did Kaitlyn at our apparent success. But then something unexpected and soul crushing happened. The confines of the portal door to the machine began to expand further and further.

"Quickly, Kaitlyn, we must make haste and evacuate!" I shouted to her above the noise.

She nodded and the two of us fled from the scene, hardly more than a few feet from the ever-expanding interdimensional portal. We looked back to watch as it consumed everything in its path— the house, the ground, even portions of the air. Thankfully, we managed to escape falling into the sinkhole of the portal.

With a sigh of relief, we saw that the portal began to collapse in on itself, but that respite was short-lived. Once it condensed into a small orb of inky blackness, it exploded outwards. Lightning burst out from the colossal portal, as did myriads of geometrically shaped monsters resembling shapes foreign to our world. The sky grew unnaturally black and we watched slack-jawed as those abominations scattered about the nearby town and heard shrieks from the denizens being attacked and eaten.

Would these abhorrent creatures continue to wreak havoc upon the world? Could they be stopped? Would they multiply? Could they now open the gate to their nether-world on their own and bring armies of monstrosities to the Earth? None of these questions had answers and we were powerless to do anything about the dreadful predicament we were now in.

Kaitlin and I stood with mouths agape, contemplating the horrors we had unleashed in this world.

THE CURSED APPEAL OF KNOWLEDGE

The stale air of the library smelled of dust and old papers, the best kind of perfume for a bookworm such as him, as he studied maps and trading routes for the millionth time, to consolidate his plan of action and pursue the feeling inside his chest.

Zachary Patel was the name, twenty four years old, and despite having a knack for fiction what truly fascinated him was the call of the abyss, the search for something more, for the invisible inherent to existence and the meaning past it all.

The year was 1884, and for lack of entertainment, and feeling repudiation for the childish games of chase that boys and girls his age used to trade in their not-so-subtle practice of wooing, his attention quickly shifted to the esteemed minds of the past. From Homer to Plato and more, a universe of knowledge and fantasy became exposed to his eyes, as what changed in manners of language and ways of conveying meaning did not change, in fact, the ways of logos and pathos, and their shimmering appeal.

It was an evening in the library not unlike this one, a few days past, when, having perused most of the fiction section of his hometown library, Zachary started wondering if there was something else, something that could fill his heart with wonder once a tolerance to the fantastic was reached, once becoming bored by the stories of dragons and knights, the likes of Don Quixote and more. The logic from books of politics and math was interesting, sure, but their knowledge was like a ladder of sorts, of which you needed memorizing the first steps in order to progress further, a practice that didn't make for a very enjoyable, light-hearted read.

Books in hand, he had finished his daily browsing of the stories the old librarian thought he could enjoy and was putting the tomes away. Clumsy as always, a piece of his pants got caught on a protruding nail as he was climbing a stool to reach the tallest shelf, forcing him to use the bookshelf itself to gain balance, causing the whole thing to menacingly shake. A noise of something falling caught his attention, almost as if an object had come loose from between the two wooden bookcases. Climbing down, he looked in the crevice, able to see nothing, but aiding his vision with a candle, a dark object was stowed away in that cramped space between the letter C and D. How to reach?

Retrieving a ruler from the librarian, it was just long enough to catch on the edge of that flat, rectangular object, fallen in the dusty hidden spot. Inch by inch, it was dragged closer, until, finally the little item was retrieved.

It appeared to be a booklet, black leather in cover and cracked by age, slightly bigger than a human hand when held flat. On the center top part, gold letters were printed like scratches, reading "Directions to the Imperial Bibliotheca - Arkham".

Immediately curious, the little item was taken to a table, his candle placed close, to provide a little more light on his find. On that cloudy evening of autumn, there was little natural light to illuminate anything, especially inside an already darkened library room.

Inside the yellowed pages stained with age, Zachary found the clumsy writing of a rushed hand, writing in violent strokes that conveyed fear and haste. The info contained therein described trade routes stopping apparently nowhere, blank signs pointing in the direction of no particular landmark or city, and lastly, several reports of erratic people found walking in the morning mist between the hours of 2:00 to 5:00 ante meridian. All this information was minutely catalogued, in a way you wouldn't think possible from someone with such bad writing, and yet there it was, triangulating the position of a mysterious location and giving it the name of "Arkham, MA".

From there, several more notes alluded to the existence of a bibliotheca of untold beauty, containing knowledge carried over the ages and dating as far back as the coveted library of Alexandria, like the collection of forbidden vexes collected in the pages of the nefarious Necronomicon.

To the chronically bored Zachary, running on empty of stories to read, that seemed like an invitation to paradise. Neglecting to finish reading the notes, the booklet was pocketed, and a plan was established.

Coming back to the present, into the familiar library, a few maps were bought and scribbled upon with circles and arrows, pointing apparently nowhere to any outside observer, and from some notes in the leather jotter a name came evident, that of a family of merchants, in their trade since generations.

Establishing contact with them was easy, and presto, a price was agreed upon with the shady figure for Zachary to be deposited at the established location. The experienced looking merchant was concealing some sort of grin under his abundant, white mustache, his eyes glimmering with malice unknown.

The convoy started its ride in the early hours of the morning, earlier than 3:00 am, when the fog was still lingering and the sun had yet to peek behind the mountains. It took no less than a couple hours for them to reach the destination agreed upon, and once there, Zachary was summoned to come out.

Picking up his backpack in haste, he hopped down from the cart, expectant and hopeful, only to be met with nothing but fog and empty land.

"What is this…? Is this the right place?", he asked the men.

"Sure is. Your destination will be in front of you", snickered the old man, with the horse's bridles in one hand, and using a tree branch he had to whip the horses to point in the midst of the morning haze.

"Are you serious? There's nothing there!", Zachary exploded, feeling scammed.

" 'Tis what you paid for. We'll be back soon to retrieve you, in case your stay bores you. Try not to have too much fun", cackled the merchant, whipping the bridles and starting the cart in a rush.

"Wait! You… cursed villain!"

The merchant was probably lying about being back, and now, Zachary was left on his own. He turned around to look at the fog, unusually swaying in slow twisters, like limbs of a concealed creature inviting him in.

"Might as well take a look", he thought, trying as best he could to rationalize the curiosity growing in his chest.

A few steps were taken before the haze was entered, as a feeling of shadows rushing past him overcame his mind, experiencing some sort of ghastly encounter with a river of souls rushing in the opposite direction as him. Confused, but no less curious, he pushed forward. One, two, three steps, as his lucidity slipped away more and more, almost swooning.

Making a final stomp to ground himself in reality, he found himself on the other side of the wall of fog, the weakness subsiding. He clapped his hands against his face to regain consciousness, and once he opened his eyes again the city presented itself to him, in horrid detail.

The mist he had come through was, in fact, pouring from the streets and the canals of the dark town, rushing in torrents of white to lift far above what was visible, blanketing the sky and the land outside with a bubble-like shroud. The cacophonous architecture gave reason to think of the secular nature of this settlement, alternating crumbling wooden structures, left to rot in their decayed state, to stone buildings by the wonderful, sturdy appeal, to ones of more modern, composite brick nature, decorated with plumes of smoke from their chimneys.

His wonder could not but grow as he walked closer, with each stone and brick in the lonely streets evoking inherent malevolence and spite, a hate for outsiders communicated to Zachary through insidiously tall towers, narrow streets and corvine roofs.

It wasn't a surprise that the streets were empty, given the cold fog running through his bones at that early time of morning, and yet, looking closer, many shadows appeared, that of pigmy like people, wearing hats and holding baskets or candles, dodging around him never to be truly in view behind the veils of mist, as they almost unconsciously avoided him for his foreign nature.

It took Zachary some hours, walking puzzled in the tortuous streets that seemed to disagreeably turn sharp angles as they wanted, to finally find himself in front of the majestic library.

The Victorian allure of this facility exuded the same austere appeal of cathedrals of yore, towering above the rest of town and wearing flying buttresses, as gowns on both sides, like legs of a stony spider. The massive gate presented a smaller door on its center, with a brass knocker hanging as a handle.

Knock Knock Knock

Zachary slammed the lion shaped knocker three times, hoping someone on the inside would come and allow him entrance, only to be met with the heavy silence of the town, only broken by the subtle gusts of wind lifting fog from the streets.

After some minutes waiting, he gave up, turned around to walk away, before an unlocking sound alerted his hearing, and a heavy door was heard creaking.

"Are you the one who's knocked?", a female voice asked.

Turning around in a startle, Zachary stuttered.

"Ah, yes, uhm, it was me indeed!"

The woman who opened the door appeared of an esteemed age, not unlike many old ladies he had seen prior, yet with a particularly sagging appearance, as if she was well into her three digits years.

"Come along then, young man", she croaked.

The insides were perhaps even more majestic, with basalt bookshelves decorated in lucid obsidian reaching the roof with delicate balance and presenting rotting ladders by their sides, patched several times over with pieces of cloth, like the bandaging of a broken limb; they looked unstable at best to climb.

The moldering tomes appeared all different in size, condition, color and even shapes, with some of round or triangular pages, and some more being as big as a table, unceremoniously laid over the very top of the shelves, looking as if they could fall at any moment.

Oil sconces adorned the sides of the stone shelves, projecting a warm light in localized spots, with heavy wooden tables in between the walkways, covered in papers and compasses or rulers. It seemed as if the place was well used by many, given the quantity of candle lights left on the tables, as no single person would likely need more than one of these flames.

Taking his eyes off the ceiling and closing his mouth, gaping wide in surprise, he asked his question to the librarian walking him through the building.

"Say, by grace, I've heard you keep here a copy of the Necronomicon, is that right?"

She cackled happily.

"Oh, my dear son, there's no such thing as a Necronomicon. Not in the real sense anyway. The book is a work of fiction.

"Fiction?" Zachary was stunned.

"Yes, it was the work of numerous science fiction and horror writers of the early 20th century who collaborated to craft a wonderfully imaginative demonic tome. We do, however, collect knowledge of similar nature, occult books that are authentic, if you're interested…"

"Y-Yes, I would be!", Zachary beeped.

She smiled softly.

"Then, let me show you…"

She walked him to a section on the back, where the shelves were cracked and partly collapsed in small piles of debris, and the sconces dark and coated in silver cobwebs. A ladder close by was taken by her, the most beaten up yet, and she climbed the entirety of it as it creaked and waved, and the noise of the cloth holding it tight could be heard ripping.

Despite that, she took her time at the very top, collecting a dark blue book and blowing on it, producing great clouds of dust. Slowly, she descended, and apologizing for her slowness due to her old bones, she delivered the book in Zachary's hands.

"Here you go, handsome", she said before walking away and leaving him to his devices.

Flirting? Zachary thought the librarian was attractive, but he never thought she'd be interested in him. Zachary watched as she left, she gave him a quick glance before turning the corner out of the book aisle. Zachary was curious about the woman's intentions, but he quickly turned his attention to more relevant matters.

The book had a title; "Spectacles of Ancient Counter-Curses" written in big, white, higher case letters, and appeared ripped and stained with use, with droplets of what looked like blood… Nah, it was probably just tea, he thought.

Collecting a candle from a table, Zachary had difficulty

finding some matches to light it, resorting to taking one of the ladders in the best conditions and simply climbing up to a sconce to catch the wick on fire. A curious fragrance emanated from the candle, it seemed to be a strange combination of satyr and frankincense.

Sitting down, Zachary gazed at the cover of the ancient and mystical tome. Its cover was leather bound and tattered and it smelled of mildew and must. As he turned the pages, many of them seemed to be written in languages he could not decipher. The Illustrations were mix of ancient and recent. Zachary concluded that different scribes may have written this book in different centuries, and then, at some point, collected as whole.

Zachary soon came upon some passages that were written on Old English and he was able to analyze them. They spoke of Old Gods and malevolent spirits that could be awakened and called upon.

More pages were turned, revealing instructions to seemingly summon entities and gain their otherworldly assistance.

A passage read *"It is thus that I pledge my heart to summon you, Bogubruzz, knight of the company of horrors and devourer of my enemies, to lay waste to whom I despise."*

Reading those words, a shiver ran down his spine, like a trickle of cold sweat from his hairline, just a second before the light of his candle went out.

Before Zachary could reach for the sconce again, a small flame burst through the darkness.

"It gets drafty in here," the librarian emerged from the shadows with a candle and proceeded to re-ignite the one that sat on the table before Zachary. She slowly leaned in as the two wicks touched each other. Zachary could smell her perfume, intoxicating lavender he surmised, her breasts seem to be more exposed now as he tried to keep his eyes from staring.

"Feel free to recite the words, they are of a beautiful ancient poetry that hasn't been spoken in decades if not centuries," she spoke as her ruby red lips seemed to hypnotize Zachary.

"Breathe in the essence," she said as she blew the smoke in Zachary's direction, already feeling a bit intoxicated, and he inhaled the spice-riddle bouquet.

With words resonating in his skull as if he was the ones speaking them, a voice from beyond erupted thunderously in his mind. It spoke in unknown and lost tongues, but to Zachary, it made perfect sense.

It demanded a sacrifice for having been summoned. It found that there was no offering for his services. His anger grew, and his voice went silent.

In an explosion of black sludge, the pages of the book ripped off as the dark gel enveloped everything around, including Zachary, in their malevolent fury. This dense slime presented teeth and closed eyelids running on its surface, and was warm to the touch like a living being, wrapping around his body as the young man struggled in vain.

Zachary was unsure if he was experiencing this for real or if it was some bizarre hallucination. He seemed to be frozen unable to react. He could see the librarian smirking, now hovering in the darkness, parts of her illuminated by the flickering candles.

"So be it! If a sacrifice is not to be presented, the summoner themselves, shall be, the sacrifice!" said the booming voice, mockingly speaking in fluent English as a last message to the trapped young man.

The black ooze slithered out from what now seemed like a hole in the pages of the cursed compendium. It created a break in the fabric of space and time, a doorway to a realm of nightmares and horror.

Zachary's arm was the first appendage to be enveloped by the dark slime as it meandered its way up to his torso. Now frozen, he could do nothing as the felt it burn its way through his skin. Like a piercing acid, the amaroidal sludge ate its way through to his bones. Like octopoidal tentacles, the mucus wrapped itself around Zachary and pulled him in.

He screamed for help as the slime retracted, slipping inside the book, turning to screams of pain once his bones were being crushed to dust in order to fit in the pages. And having one last scream, his skull was crushed too, just as the slime completely disappeared inside, re-assembling all the ripped pages to their original position and swinging closed.

The librarian, emerging from the obscurity of the dark, placed her hand on the top of the book and smiled. Her work was done, at least for the moment. *Bogubruzz* had been appeased.

She picked up the cursed grimoire and returned it to its original position, ready to lure in more ignorant fools that were stupid enough to wander in without a protection from vexing.

The librarian, snickering, took another sip of her horrid, rat-infused tea, before going back to her duties of dusting and sorting.

She would soon have another appointment with a curious patron and needed to be sure there was no visible evidence of tonight's incident.

AN ACCOUNT OF OZGAMUUN

I came into possession of my uncle's condo apartment just outside of Milomee's Stand last summer. I wasn't sure what to make of the occasion. I didn't know my uncle well, and I'd venture to say none of us truly did, at least not in his final years. He drifted away from the family when I was still a young boy. He was a man from the old country, a more distant relative than merely "uncle" but he held a special place in our family for reasons that were only ever explained to me.

I found the apartment to be well stocked and handsomely furnished. Most of his things were still in, though they were promised to others and I was not to use or sell them in the interim. It was all part of the will he left and I'm not now or was then a cruel enough person to dishonor a dead man's words. It was a nice break away from the usual grind of my life just outside of Albany. A bit northern for my liking, but it was still the summer. An extra place to stay half the year wasn't a bad take.

I stayed there for a few months until the first winter storms were about to hit. In that time, many people visited to lay claim to some of uncle's items. No one I recognized, not from the family or even nearby. They all seemed to have travel on their minds and spoke of him very little. That is, until one certain man came named Felix Urist Strovsgard, an old but strong looking Swedish man with a bulbous nose and a big smile. He was here for something specific, an item that was requisitioned into its own room even before I arrived.

A chest, huge and wooden with reliefs of old Viking men hauling great treasure across its sides. I never opened it, never cared to, and told Mr. Strovsgard the same, and his reaction surprised me. He asked if I'd like to take a look inside before he left. In truth, I wanted to, but thought better of myself and politely declined him. He asked if he could stay for a bit while his driver returned with a bigger car. Mostly, he wanted to speak of my uncle. I put on some coffee and served it with the intent to listen.

He asked me, "How long have you stayed here in Larens' old home?" His English was good, but his accept was thick. I could make out what he said if only because nothing else was distracting my mind. I told him it had been a few months and he nodded. Then he looked at the chest. "You ever hear odd knocking at strange hours?"

I admitted that I hadn't, but that I'm not a quiet person in my own right. I often pass my time with music or TV between my work. "It'd be a shame not to tell you then," he began. "Your uncle Laurens was a bit of a wicked man. I do not mean to disrespect him in front of you, as he was family of yours, and no doubt you've mourned him properly, but we knew him as something else."

I agreed that I didn't know him, but hearing the accounts, I wished to. He offered me a deal then, to be finished weeks later. He said he had my uncle's journal, a log of events he kept during his time in Sweden up until the time he passed. None of us ever saw him after he died. We were told his remains were interred abroad as well, though he never renounced any citizenship, his last remaining will and testament was to be upheld. His only possessions in the end were kept for him in the place he died, a hamlet town of Hvanhólar up in the northern reaches.

I accepted his trade, though I saw it as more of a kindness. I even helped him with the trunk out to the back of the flatbed that pulled up. When we loaded it up, and as I secured it for him in the back, I heard and felt a knocking coming from inside. It rapped on the wood with force. When Mr. Strovsgard heard it he could only chuckle. "You're either deaf or a kind liar to hear none of this the whole time it's been with you!"

He laughed, not to mock me, but I suppose at whatever memory he had of uncle Laurens still remained in that chest. Something moving, something loose and knocking around. Nothing to bother me. I tied it up and saw him go, and a few weeks later I received a package at the apartment's address. I had it forwarded to me in my winter home near Albany and saw it was addressed from Sweden, out of the Gothenberg area. It was about the shape and weight of a book, as promised.

The diary looked older than it should have, like a hand-me-down from an era past. The name on the front was my uncle's, but the title was not his own. It was a simple note taking book, a journal for personal use, but he'd inscribed it in dark ink as *The Account of Ozgamuun, His Summoning, and His Powers as witnessed by Laurens van Ginneken*. A novel name for his last written biography. I read through it on the day I received it during an early winter snowstorm.

~~~

I, in my fair state of mine, have met with an impasse in my studies. The matters of the occult, passed down to me in honor and reverence by the black historians of old, have led to a conclusive finding on the matter of the summoning of the demon Ozgamuun. Nazi files and cold war pilferings have given way to the extradited remains of a certain acolyte whose burial was untraced but well defined that scioned the demon into this world at the expense of his body. It acts, still, as a vessel to commune and control the demon's power. I must seek it out and wield that power for myself!

My trail has led me into Sweden. The frozen north of this country hides many secrets. Old cults rose up once in ancient times. When man walked alongside the mammoths and the European lions of old he did not struggle alone. There were forces at work in the icy heights at the roof of the world to help them. Elden Gods of strength and power.

Ozgamuun is close. His sigil is seen in many places and his name is spoken in secret hushes. There is a ceremony to honor the old ones that I must attend. My credentials as an occult researcher do not hold sway. I must offer them something, anything for an audience. If Ozgamuun heeds me, whatever I offer, I may get back.

Success! I have joined in the solstice march! They trace the path of mankind's ancestors who wandered far and struggled hard to pray in homage to the Elder Gods of the hinterlands. Ozgamuun is close and his summoning shall be at hand. I have been asked to make a sacrifice of my self. They have not instructed me fully of what I must do, but I shall perform for them in any way I can to maintain their trust.

Our procession began in minimal clothing. I was given the opportunity as an outsider to bring my journal along to record the events for my own posterity. I hold no allegiance to any state or sponsor or university. I am a man propelled exclusively by his own desires to connect with the Elder Gods, to harness their powers. I wish to discover the fate of the fallen acolyte and correct his failed course of being if I can.

The march led us up high into the hills of a fjord where a glacial passage ran through and created a deep, narrow valley. The waters of the arctic flowed around the passage and rarely in. the ocean itself seemed to spite the very land below and refused to fill it willingly. Great dams were constructed not to maintain the stagnancy of the dried valley but to connect the stranded island hillside to the mainland.

The works were ancient, older than the furthest village from civilization, but remarkably sound. It was as though I walked upon the constructs of a culture that was above the techniques we considered modern building. Such is Ozgamuun's power! The one who lifted up early man to rise above his competitors in the mythic era of Neanderthal warring. The One Before All!

We arrived at the worship site. A circle of risen stone pillars awaited us. A Stonehenge which may in fact predate the one of much fame on the British Isles. Both were druidic in nature, monuments raised in worship to a power beyond the builder's purview and power to understand. Were it only so easy to prove. Approach of the stones as forbidden, for they were the gate and the cell, the prison and the key. I maintained distance from them out of reverence, but I would give a soul or more to just run my hands upon them.

At the bottom of a steep climb of stairs I watched the members of the circle descend their went one by one into the dry abyss. Though the days were long, the shadow was dark. The wall of earth we stood on that parted the seas offered no merciful glimpse to the bottom from the top we stood on. To know, one had to descend. They allowed me to observe, but not to participate beyond that.

Those who went down did not return. The congregation threw their hands up in an offered prayer. I have transcribed the prayer   as   thus:
Let us release from our selves and find the Self. The one who we are, the One Before All, may he find our Truth and hold it Higher.

The purpose of the rituals, as I observed, was to offer the old and the feeble to the Earth once more in reverence to forgotten halcyon past. I asked for clarity, to know what lied at the bottom even if I could not observe it, but was rebuked at all turns. It is not for prying eyes, I was told. If I looked too long, my eyes would crawl out of my body. Sheer mockery. I could not stand it!

I have decided to embark on the journey myself. I am not yet old enough to meet their standards for death, but I shall not die. I aim to return, to observe the demon where it lies, as a crater of a fae meteor or the corpse of an exhumed dinosaur, I care not. I wish to see it and know what power it holds.

The trek was harder than before. A storm rose up to impede me but it did not work. I found my way back to the hidden valley as I had done before and found my way to the sturdy bridges that crossed high above the secret pit below. My view was blocked by the snowstorm, but my footing was solid.

The pillars were my first and most important part of research. I could not feel them as closely as I wanted. The storm was at its most intense when I reached the henge. It was a terror, as though the forces of the world itself sought to keep my driven away from my discovery.

The rocks were soft. I could press my hiking pick into them and leave a dent, which pushed back on its own in time.

Springy but rigid, like great wads of flesh.

The climb down was more treacherous. Even with my climbing gear I battled against a storm, a sheer drop, and my own age. I began a descent downward to the abyss. I had to know what legacy awaited. The body of the great demon Ozgamuun awaited me!

~~~

I looked up to my own room and stared around curiously. I felt the chill of the cold air from outside creeping in as I read. The account of my uncle, and his odd brush with a twisted fate concluded there for the time. There were more pages, but my mind felt strained at the prospect of continuing. It seemed that Mr. Strovsgard had mixed intentions when he sent me the journal. It wasn't for the purpose of a kindly family reunion with my uncle's lost expedition. This was an account of a sin. Defilement of a sacred site, betrayal of the trust of a community who welcomed and accepted him.

I learned enough about my uncle that night and let the book rest on my reading table until the next day. That night, curiously, I heard a knocking at the door. It was late at night, and all my reasoning was scattered. I took my gun from my nightstand just in case. At worst I considered that it could be a wandering homeless person trying to pry for attention or ask for a meal even charity had its limits, though.

Through the eyehole I saw no one. I kept looking, to try and catch an angle of someone waiting nearby, but saw nothing. And then as I looked, I heard the knock again, right up against my own skull that was so close to the door. A knocking on my door with no owner. Not a single thing in sight. Knocking, just like in the trunk of uncle's possession. What else had he done? What secrets still existed?

The book had to have more. I was tempted to flip to the end but my own fingers betrayed me in that. My body, and my mind, wanted to read on from where I left off. If I learned too soon what he'd done and saw the end I would not know if the demon he sought was real either. I was more curious about that than the phantasmal knocking at that moment.

I sat again, as the storm outside built up and the knocking faded away, to read.

~~~

The bottom of the abyss was safe from the storm. It raged overhead like a sheet thrown above my head but I had surpassed it. My pick slid through the soft dirt of the fjord's hillside and lowered me down with grace into a shallow tar pit. The ground was an ichor of ancient slime left to decay in the open air for eternity.

In the center of the mass I saw something rising out of the muck, half stuck in the swampy black ooze and faded into an off-yellow hue, like a great-calcified bone. As I approached the smell hit me. It was the scent of thousands of deaths, and the most recent were still rotting. I saw their arms detached from their bodies and their forms all splayed out in naked death and recline. The tar ate them before their own bodies could. A force greater than death took them. A demon.

I witnessed Ozgamuun there and knew for the first time that it was he. The many-rounded toothy growth from the ooze had a faint heartbeat that I could feel through my glove. When I pulled away I saw some of the fuzz of my glove was pricked off and left behind as a soft dark stain on its surface.

This bone, or tooth, or gnarled growth still lived. The ooze puckered against its sides like a low tide went swirling around the base. The bodies moved as I watched on, very slightly, and drifted apart. I knew not how, and no clues remained. Whatever the travellers did during this ritual, it ended with their deaths.

I tried to observe the detached arms of one of the elder gentlemen who descended just the other day. Through the muck I could see the arm was emaciated and shriveled up. It was the arm of an old man, for certain, but it was also drained of every bit of moisture that could have kept it in a healthy looking shape.

The hand of an arm, detached into the muck, twitched. It twitched! It moved, fingers curling and reaching out! It was gone at the elbow, just an upper arm and hand, but it moved. I saw it all clearly. No snow interfered with my vision, and my nose was masked from the fermented stench. They moved! They lived!

I struck a guess as to what could have happened. It was the great protrusion, the hideous mound of tooth that grew from the ground. An ancient belonging of a far larger creature, or perhaps its own true self, conscious and sealed within a calcium casket of its own making. The ways of demons are unclear to me, even in my occult research, for I have never seen one such as this in depictions of any culture.

I took a daring guess and placed my naked hand onto the surface of the tooth. At that moment, I felt myself transported far away and long into the past. I saw reaching fields of short grass, rich greens and wide rolling mountains of deep brown in the distance. I saw through time to an age of men and mammoths between the great snowfalls that covered the Earth in perpetual frost and ice.

When the vision ended I was returned to the world and the storm above was over. I was left face up in the tar. My coat peeled away from me when I sat up, but otherwise I was fine. I felt better than fine. My body felt regenerated, like I'd taken a long and warm rest beyond my own expectations.

If you see these entries afterwards be different or changed, it is because I lack the means to write properly any longer. My right arm has turned extremely numb. However, this has not been a lossy venture on my part. Though my arm is lost, I have acquired immense power.

My studies in the occult ritual invoked a response from the Swedish government. I've been granted amnesty and a residence in Gothenberg. The government has managed to safehouse me against a building force of rural opposition claiming that I have defaced their land. They prosecute me for seeking knowledge. I am a hero to the ignorant and hated by the enlightened. And for that I am rewarded.

My right arm is now lost to me. It no longer responds even to my will to leave it limp. It has begun moving against my will. I still cannot feel it, and the doctors I have counseled with have confirmed my worst suspicions, that the blood in my body is being rejected. It's swollen up and hardened across the surface. They say it is bloat evidenced in drowning. The surface is smooth, like enamel.

I have managed without my right arm for one month. I have told no one about it and even lied to a ring of doctors on how it was removed and by whom. No medical records will be kept. Only this, the testament of Ozgamuun, must contain the truth. For the arm remains in my possession, and just like those who surrendered to the embrace of the demon, it still lives with a will of its own. I have locked it in a cedar trunk for the time being. I will see how long it can last outside of its intended habitat.

The arm has become its own entity, and unliving, virulent thing. I check on it rarely, as it springs itself to life once it knows I am tumbling the lock. It is almost like it is aware of me. Like it can hear, or sense my presence. However, what I've learned from it directly link it to the workings of Ozagmuun. And they correlate to the boons I have incurred. I must test this theory further. As the arm lives and grows stronger, the friendships I've made without effort have also grown. My recognition grows the longer I keep this secret held.

I have now done the impossible. For many, the unthinkable. I have tamed the will of the demon Ozgamuun and learned its origin. I initiated a second expedition to the site with the aid of Swedish militants. The pillars were missing, but the demon remained. The tar, and the tooth which makes it, are one in the same, a continuous, split entity, which turns organisms into semblances of itself and absorbs their material. The offerings help it grow, and only the brave can gain its favor with their living sacrifices. Long has it waited for an acolyte such as I, not to be devoured, but to use its power willingly.

It has been too long since my thoughts were recorded, and since the movements of the demon were accounted for. Something blasphemous occurred, which I was unable to stop. An attempt was made to extract the demon from its resting place, to pull the tooth from the black pitch that surrounded it. They tried with a helicopter, the only thing they could to reach it in that harrowing valley, but it crashed. It was a soft crash, the pilot survived, but the rescue team watched from above as he crawled through the tar and was eaten. Soon after, his body parts were separated and consumed by the tar, and all of them kept moving. His arms and legs and torso, his organs from within it, his head, all-alive but separate, and motivated to spread by the demon's will. Just like my arm.

I must retreat from Sweden. It is unsafe here. Though, I will not go without aide. I have resolved to give up my second arm. I'll even surrender my legs if I have to. To walk from Ozgamuun is to invite its blessings into your life, this I am certain of. For my first arm, he gave me power. For the second he will give me riches to survive with. For the first leg, the comforts of a home and love exclusive to only me. For my last leg, immortality. The demon's power will be mine. Before they flood the valley and wash its influence out into the vastness of the ocean, I shall take as much power as I can into the world!

~~~

The book ended there. The knocking continued. I was awash with uncertainty, but the night grew late and the knocking stayed loud. I went to check, gun in one hand, book in the other, and cracked the door open.

I saw an arm lying on the ground. Just an arm. It twitched. It seemed to be reaching and grasping for something. It seemed to want for something that it knew I had. So I handed down the book. The arm, bulging and puffed up like a baby's arm, but sized to an adult's length, took the book from me and started to pull itself away. I saw it travel across the walkway and off into the night. I also saw, across the street, a collection of body parts lingering just within the view of the streetlights before they all hobbled and rolled independent of one another back away.

That was the last I saw of my distant uncle Laurens van Ginneken. I wonder often if old Mr. Strovsgard truly was a friend of his, one of the many who his influence reached from the font of power the demon granted him. Or if he was one of the cultists my uncle wronged to take from their relic of power before it was lost to them forever. Perhaps he wanted uncle out of hiding and knew he'd find the book faster than he'd find me.

And I wonder, even now, if the mound and tar known as Ozgamuun was still out there, floating as a heap on the ocean floor. And if someone were to find it, what would it give them to be free again?

THAT WHICH LURKS

The fascination that has gripped humanity ever since it had first begun traversing across the Earth was the notion of sentient, all-powerful entities who ruled above them. These wildly wondrous, beauteous, and omnipotent beings were, of course, used to light and guide the way for the unilluminated minds of humanity not privy to the truths of the cosmos, space, and time. Man attributed all that natural phenomena that they witnessed to be due to the intercession of celestial hands giving graces or curses as they saw fit.

This animistic way of thinking had and still does to some extent reveal how a man views the universe around him, albeit in a much more evolved fashion in this day and age. For example, it was not long before stories of specific gods had sprung up within different cultures spread out across the world. Whether it be the story of Prometheus who stole fire from The Olympian rulers and gave it to humanity for their use. Or how Ahuramazda would eventually prevail over his antagonist Angra Mainyu and live in eternal bliss with his righteous followers. Quite similar to those who believe in Yahew and numerous other deities and creator gods in fact.

How did the transition from viewing the natural world as being characterized and controlled by mischievous spirits and minor supernatural beings to all-mighty and illustrious divine creators and destroyers? Even with the written recordings of the earliest religions and other texts that have survived through the passage of time are not satisfactory in answering this question. For, it would be an erroneous conclusion to come to, when it is without a doubt that man has worshipped supreme beings who have not been recorded. Or passed down orally from the mouths of storytellers within their respective places of origin.

Therefore, the question yet still remains unanswered. The switch from animistic worship, the belief that souls residing within plants and inanimate objects organize and animate the seen and unseen phenomena of the cosmic landscape. To, of course, godhead's who set everything in motion through their high intelligence and unmatched organizational skills. Acquiring followers by the billion, who trust in them implicitly or even with a healthy amount of skepticism.

Some say that it is all nonsense, just humanity screaming out into the abyss, hoping for salvation that is dulled out by random. This idea is vehemently opposed by many men as agreeing with it would cause unwelcome existential dread and leave one depressed beyond repair. If all that is done on the whim of mathematical probability and uncaring forces that govern all of reality, then why even consider that one is special or unique at all?

These philosophical and religious questions have been hotly debated and even warred over by different factions of humanity who hope and pray that their way is correct. Whether out of genuine faith or by the refusal to relent to another's viewpoint, no one knows which option is selected more often than not.

Perhaps the original progenitors of animism and organized faith would be able to answer such questions and caused them to first believe in unearthly forces.

The one man who wishes to discover the original thoughts of ancient mankind was none other than Sir Robert Doleman, a historian and excellent theologian hailing from New York City, but born from English parents. Graduated at the ripe age of twenty from the prestigious Columbia University with incredible marks, graduating two years early. A young man of excellent looks, spirit, and mind as thought so by all who knew him, but suffered from frequent bouts of illness. Who, regardless of his many duels with sickness, traveled around the world speaking to not members of the major faiths, but the cult-like ones.

The first of his many trips brought him to Greece, where he gained knowledge of the Cult of Cybele, or Magna Mater from a museum in Athens. It was here he learned about the great Cybele and how she was worshipped in the fifth century BCE. She had the honor of being a goddess of fertility, healing, and a protector during times of war. She was always accompanied by large and foreboding lions, ruling over the entirety of the world on top of mountains, overseeing all with her knowing gaze. Cybele often carried a primitive version of a tambourine, which she urged her followers to use; alongside other percussive instruments to sing her praises and worship her with. Of course, dancing was involved for the goddess to complement the frantic playing of instruments.

However, What Sir Doleman noted that was rather disturbingly ironic and disgusting to his senses was a certain ritual that was known as the Taurobolium. A sordid and depraved ritual that caused gasps to be expelled from the lungs of poor Sir Doleman in awe of what the resident historian of the museum related to him.

"Those wanting to join the Cult of Cybele had to undergo the Taurobolium in order to be accepted. These initiates had to lay beneath a bull, bodies spread out, not covering their faces especially and wait." The Greek historian explained.

"And what did they wait for?" Sir Doleman asked, concerned at what he may hear next.

"The priests would ritualistically slaughter the chosen bull, spilling the blood in a ghastly fashion onto the initiates." The man would go on to explain that the initiates had to accept every drop of crimson blood that was poured over them, bathing in those life juices. Utterly confused by the stark contrast of Cybele as a goddess of fertility and healing and her bloody initiation ritual. Why would a protector goddess demand blood be spilled and cover her followers with death?

Sir Doleman was distressed deeply by such things and asked the historian to elaborate further on the personality and nature of Cybele. The bespectacled man whispered for the young graduate to follow him to his private office to speak further.

Once the two had settled in the musty and dusty little room, Sir Doleman received his answer.

"Cybele was a particularly nasty entity, yet was loved by many all those years ago. Those who followed her believed they would in turn be resurrected for their devotion?"

"What sort of devotion did she demand, good sir?" Sir Doleman inquired, pulling a notepad and pen from his satchel. The elderly historian held his tongue for a moment, seemingly debating whether or not to share, before going against his better judgment and telling Doleman what he knew.

"Cybele once tried to be a mortal, Attis. And when he rejected her lover, she cursed him with dark madness and the man castrated himself. Of course, he was later revived, but the followers of her believe if they too castrate themselves, they will attain resurrection and immortality." He paused briefly before leaning in and speaking in a much more frightened tone. "Based on my own research...she was something dark, a reprobate, a sanctimonious entity playing with mankind for her own unknown pleasures. What she is...is old, a great old beast, that I am certain. She still has followers, hidden from sight that still perform her ritual but no longer use bulls...but humans instead I do not know more than that. Now, please leave." Doleman tried to ask for clarification as this was the knowledge he had never heard in his life but was rebuffed by the frightened man in front of him. He was then ushered out quickly and told to never speak to anyone what he told him, and that he only told this to Doleman to clear his conscience of the wicked things he had chanced upon.

While frustrated by the abrupt end to the conversation, Doleman left satisfied with the debased knowledge he had gained. However, he began to wonder what the historian meant when he talked about the true nature of Cybele and if it was truly humanity who had originated the concept of animism or things of divine nature. Curious for more answers, Doleman set out for the ancient land of Canaan and talked amongst the learned men of Israel, Palestine, Syria, and Lebanon.

It was his research here that brought to light the ancient Canaanite religion and one such deity named Moloch, the god of fire. He learned it was an anthropomorphic deity with the body of a man and the head of a bull, also called the Great King. It was to him did the ancient Canaanites sacrifice their children through fire and war. He learned with despicable detail how children of the youngest of ages would be tossed into burning idols of that deity, alive. Ritualistically killed in order to gain the blessing of the Great King.

When Doleman asked how did this blasphemous practice begin or what inspired the Canaanites to do it, he was met with averted gazes and awkward stances from the learned men he encountered. Each and every one of them refused to answer further, showing Doleman that many of them knew something terrible to some degree. While Doleman was certain they were afraid of telling him deplorable truths, he knew that what they did know was incomplete. Same as the historian from Greece, only knowing of tiny bits of details that stalled their research into such things.

However, just when Doleman was about to give up his endeavors after traveling around the world for nearly a decade, he had struck gold. During a trip to Eastern Russia, he happened upon an old mystic. A crazed man who happened to hear Doleman asking around with a guide about local religions or cults. He wildly came upon Doleman, smelling of sweat, dung, and other torrid smells.

He talked rapidly to Doleman for several minutes before clapping his hands and miming himself turning a page in a book before running away suddenly. Doleman asked what on Earth the man was saying to his guide, who looked considerably distressed.

"He said that if you wanted answers to all things concerning the universe, the unwritten past of humanity, and what set us about this path, he should seek out the Necronomicon. A book filled with arcane knowledge and sorcery that belonged to man known as Alhazred, or the Mad Arab. In that book, will you find all that you wish to know." Doleman, struck with the memory of hearing of this text from his professors back at Columbia, determined to return at once and ask his former mentor, John Phillips about it.

Without rest on his arrival home, Doleman sought out

Professor Phillips and questioned him on what he knew about the Necronomicon.

"Oh, that old thing? Why would you ever want to know about some...book that entertained nonsense such as 'magic' and 'secret' information?" Phillips scoffed and downed a glass of brandy while pouring another out of courtesy for Doleman, who declined.

"It is for my research, sir. Surely you have heard of this text from somewhere or someone?" Doleman asked, hopeful that his journey may finally bear fruit. The professor sighed deeply, rolling his eyes.

"Why? What urges you to pursue such things as this? Trust me, my boy, fervently studying religion and philosophy to unlock something that you perceive as groundbreaking will drive you mad or make you a laughing stock by your peers." Phillips, wanting to prevent his protégé from becoming seen with eyes of derision said this as a courtesy to Doleman. Frustrated by this, however, Doleman stood up and pulled his textbook collection worth of notes from his satchel and slammed down on Phillips's desk.

"I did not travel across this godforsaken planet to come here and become ridiculed for my efforts, sir. With all due respect at least take the time to hear what is that I have learned during my time amongst men both greater and lesser than us in mind." Phillips looked up at Doleman, surprised at the sudden burst of anger from his former student, slightly impressed at how assertive he had become and agreed to hear him out.

Doleman related to his mentor how each and every minor religion and cult and the major ones of the world had an unsettling trait shared amongst them all.

"Regardless of their stance as an entity of benevolence or

not, every deity had shown the capacity for wickedness that went against their nature. Those who were protectors, saviors, and just creators demanded bloodshed, violence, and chaos in order to please them. And should they be rejected, they cursed humanity with plagues, famine, madness, and death. Furthermore, the origins to their depraved and grotesque rituals are relatively unknown. Which begs the question, was humanity influenced or...coerced to commit these heinous acts by an outside force? Answer me that Professor." Doleman crossed his arms and was panting slightly due to his fast spoken rant. Phillips squinted his eyes, processing what he was just told before shrugging and tossing up his hands in defeat.

"Very well, clearly you have raised some...interesting questions about the world in which we live. Tell you what, I did indeed hear of the Necronomicon from a former colleague of mine. He too had similar ideas as yours, albeit yours are far more succinct and easier to understand. I believe he spoke of that text and odd religions who worshipped odd beings with peculiar names like...Yog...something or another." He pulled out a pen and paper and scribbled down a name and address and handed it to me.

"His name is Jacob Reid, a short, red-haired man nearing his seventies. At one point in time he was considered as having the greatest mind in the realm of theology and history of our generation. That is until he made a trip to the Arabian Peninsula and when he returned he seemed to be infected with an inane desire to study the occult. It is for that reason I tried to assuage you of your research, fearing it would lead to an obsession that would mirror his own." Phillips leaned back in his chair and asked if Doleman had any further questions or things to share with him.

"No, sir. I thank you for your time and warning." Doleman extended his hand and Phillips shook it firmly, smirking slightly.

"Just promise me you will bring back an in-depth research report detailing all the discoveries you may make. Hell, maybe you will bring that old fool Reid back to his senses."

"You have got yourself a deal, Professor Phillips." The two then parted ways and Doleman went back to his apartment for the first time in years, dusting off his study table and setting down his numerous notes down with a thud. Finally, after all of the years of his search did he gain a lead? Not only that, but he had high hopes that he may speak with a man unafraid to speak his mind about what he knows. But, that would have to come in the morning. His tired body had endured much hardship over his travels, facing illness at every turn and so decided to rest for some odd weeks before contacting the infamous Professor Reid.

***

Once Doleman regained his strength and the illness that plagued his lungs and throat had passed, he set to work to prepare his notes to put into a letter. He was deeply concerned about failing to make a wonderful first impression on the famed Professor Reid. He had no idea as to what kind of man he was, other than that he was thought of to be a loon by his contemporaries. So, he consulted his mentor yet again as to how he should go about corresponding with the occult obsessed Reid.

"If you must know, he has a penchant for arcane artifacts, perhaps talking to him about the so-called Necronomicon will capture his interest in your work?" Phillips took a bite of his eggs, looking askance at the menu in front of him, much to the chagrin of Doleman.

"Thank you for your advice. I understand that you think

little of my work, or as flights of fantasy, but I do appreciate the help." Phillips nodded.

"Honestly, I figured you would have thought of that on your own, ha-ha. Nervous?" Phillips, teased. Doleman smiled and shook Phillips's hands before saying his goodbye and made great haste back to his apartment and wrote up a letter for old Professor Reid, which read as follows.

Hello and good tidings, Professor Reid.

I am Robert Doleman, and I have acquired your postal address thanks to an old acquaintance of yours by the name of John Phillips, an excellent scholar, and professor from Columbia University. You see, he tells me that you are fairly well-acquainted with archaic and little known religions of the world. Although, forgive him as he cares little about it and almost prevented us from communicating in the first place!

I come to you with great interest in such things, as I am a student of religion and history myself. I have traveled far and wide across the Earth, researching cults and the like. Across my many travels, I have stumbled upon word of an ancient text named the Necronomicon. This book as I have heard from Professor Phillips not only exhibits magic but also information about things mankind has not been privy to at large. I write to you in the hopes that you may help illuminate me on this text and any other information you would be willing to share with me.

Kind Regards,

Robert Doleman.

It was with an anxious heart that Doleman sent this letter with some of his notes to Professor Reid. He feared that the reclusive old man would scantily look at the letter and toss it in the trash, or burn it out of shame for his status as a madman.

Yet Doleman told himself to relax, lest he befall another duel with illness, one he felt would degrade and slow his progress in his search for answers.

His concerns turned out to be for naught in the end as one cloudy and misty, warm July morning, with great joy he noticed that he received a letter from the elderly Reid.

Hello, Mr. Doleman!

How excited I am to hear of another who shares my interest in things that many believe to be foolish scraps for learned men! And yes, I am aware of Phillips, peh! Do not let his disregard for your studies and musings discourage you. Nor allow his doughty exterior fool you; Phillips knows more about me and my work than he lets on. It is from a place of agitation that he rejects such ideas to allow his mind to rest in comfort.

I am delighted that he allowed us to be able to speak to one another, despite that. Now then, allow me to reveal to you the background as it were for the legendary Necronomicon you have heard about in frantic ramblings and cautious whispers. The book itself is leather-bound, and the letters within are a stygian-black and written in Aramaic by its author Alhazred, or the Mad Arab. Where he acquired such knowledge is yet unknown but what is known is that he was ripped and torn to shreds in a bazaar by an unknown force. I hypothesize it was an entity that helped him acquire the knowledge, but the Mad Arab must have called down its anger upon himself for some transgression or another.

But, I implore you, Mr. Doleman, to come and visit me at my mansion in the countryside of Northern England! There we can research together, funded by my own wealth, and talk at length about our shared interests.

Best,

J. Reid.

Doleman was consumed with happiness at the letter and saw that an address had been scribbled on the backside of it. Clearly being the home of Professor Reid. He then quickly drafted a letter saying he would accept the offer to research with the elderly gentleman. Once done, he promptly packed his belongings and set to work to travel to England.

***

In front of Doleman stood an enormous mansion, encapsulated by healthy and sturdy green vines that choked the red brick beneath them. At the center of the place was a tall stained glass window of myriads of different colors.

Before he could knock, the door swung open, and out came Professor Reid. He was rather short in stature, wiry frame, wrinkled face, but had full and lush red hair like that of a youth's. The two men introduced themselves and immediately sat down in Reid's living room, which was decorated with dozens of artifacts from the globe over.

It was not long before Reid began his spiel on the numerous and terrible things he had learned from his time spent in the Middle East. Of course, this was about the many deeds and dark things that have been done with the Necronomicon, but it caught all of Doleman's attention. However, something bothered him greatly.

"Ah, Professor Reid, forgive me but...where did the source of such power for this book come from? How could such things even be possible? What else...did you learn?" Reid's happy expression melted away, and he shook his head.

"Yog-Sothoth." A surge of pain shot through Doleman's head at the word.

"Pardon me? What did you say?" He asked, holding his head.

"An incorrect pronunciation is what I said. It is the name of something deeply profane and sacrilegious to all that we know, Mr. Doleman. It is spoken of numerous times within the Necronomicon and it is an entity with which we will be dealing with. While its shape and form are not known to mankind, its deeds are." Reid stood up and wandered over to an opaque glass cabinet as he explained this. He opened it and took out a large, crudely stitched together leather book. The Necronomicon.

"You...you have the book?" Doleman stood up in surprise.

"Oh yes, indeed I do. Do you want to know why I came back home with fantasies and my mind obsessed with the occult, Mr. Doleman?" Doleman stood silent, unable to process what was unfolding. "Well, I too found such studies...distasteful and a crude waste of time for men such as ourselves. That is until my wife died. She had come along with me on my trip and met a grizzly end." He stared down at the book in his hands, running a hand across the face of it.

"I'm so sorry...any man who would-" Reid shot a look of abject rage at Doleman, catching his tongue.

"It was no man who did this to my beloved Beatrice. The 'things' that ensnared her and dissected her like a common lab mouse were crustaceous, bestial things with foul-smelling fungal growths that littered their bodies! All of this research...all of it is to bring back my Beatrice. Will you aid me in this, Mr. Doleman?" Reid handed the text over to the puzzled Doleman, who looked at him in disbelief.

"Mr. Reid...with all due respect I think you need to seek aid for your mind. Tragedy often causes the mind to go soft." He said gently as he could and handed the book back to Reid. "Forgive me, I should go. I think our goals do not align after all." Doleman turned to leave, but before he could grab his belongings, Reid managed to stop him with his silvery tongue.

"You want to know the origins of all things. That book will allow us to summon the deity who can answer that question. And more. All I ask is for your aid." Doleman bit his tongue, and turned to face the old man.

"Do not take me for a fool, Mr. Reid. I am not so engrossed in my own research to believe anything that passes before my eyes and ears. But, yes, I am interested in the question as to what influenced and coerced humanity all those years ago. And yes, I want to know how all of this! All of this came to be! But do not drag me down to your madness!" Doleman shook his head and paused before apologizing for his outburst.

"Not to worry. Your concerns are valid. However, perhaps you may come to trust me after I show you a trinket I acquired years ago. Come with me." The elderly Reid turned and walked into an adjacent room and feeling as though he did not really have a choice at this point, Doleman followed. He paused, however, when he saw an enormous painting that draped the wall in front of him. Witnessing the painting made his brain feel as though it were being invaded by an unearthly and spectral force that was snaking its way around. Yet in some strange way, he found himself drawn to the abomination before him.

"What...is this?"

"That my dear boy is the form of the name I had given to you minutes earlier, yet I hesitate to say that name again for reasons I'm sure you understand." The two stared in silence at the monstrosity on the thick parchment that Reid painted upon. What they beheld was a colorful and tangled mass of color and bulbous orbs that glowed. To anyone viewing it would believe it to be nothing more than a mystifying painting of bubbles. But, Doleman knew there was far more to this than that.

"I have seen dreams, more and more frequent as the years have passed of an entity resembling these...soapy looking orbs. I see it watching, waiting from across the veil. It resides not in darkness but of a putrid place of its dimension, unable to leave. Whether by choice or not, I don't know. But I know that it is calling for me, Mr. Doleman. This is only my own conjecture, but I believe it to be one of the Great Old Ones. One of the progenitors of our creation. I tried painting it but cannot totally recall its appearance. And whenever I think I do, I find my hand and my mind to seize as though in mortal terror of what would be created." Reid then patted Doleman on the back and asked how he now felt about joining him.

"This is truly incredible, but I do not find what I would gain from helping you bring back your wife? If such a thing is possible."

"Ha, Mr. Doleman, you disappoint me. After all that you have heard and learned over your travels, you now find yourself doubting the authenticity of my claims? Allow me to share with you one more thing. The being that we shall summon using the Necronomicon possesses forbidden knowledge that will be imparted to you if you ask. All that which the cosmos has hidden from humanity will be revealed to you. Everything concerning the past, present, and future will be granted to you. This is not an opportunity I think you should let pass you by." Reid then motioned for Doleman to join him again in the other room and settled down once again in their chairs.

"I admit that this is all very tempting. But I am gravely concerned that this is an incredibly dangerous and foreboding thing you ask of me to do. After all, was it not Alhazred himself, the maker of this accursed text who had his blood spilled in a way most gruesome for his dabbling in the occult arts?" Reid raised an eyebrow and smirked. "What? Do you not care for the possible consequences of our actions?" Doleman asked, slightly incensed.

"Alhazred was a fool, a barbarian who trifled with forces that he could never possibly understand like learned men such as ourselves. Do you honestly think those of the past can barter with the gods of the cosmos and that of science?"

"Will we not be those men after we pass, Mr. Reid?" Reid smiled wide at that question.

"I was right to bring you here. But, we are digressing here. You need not be afraid of the consequence that befell Alhazred. For I have something that he did not, an artifact from a bygone era created by those long since dead." Bemused by this, Doleman asked to see such a thing and asked how it would protect them.

From his smoking jacket pocket, Reid pulled out an amber-colored stone that resembled a small, leafless branch. Inscribed on the stone were words written in a language either so old it has never been discovered or one that was alien to the world. A curious little trinket.

"What I possess here is said to ward off all that would attempt to corrupt or slaughter us. I have not transcribed the words, as I am unable to. But, from my most recent trip to Ireland, it is said this artifact is very effective in its purpose.' Reid tossed the artifact over to Doleman who inspected it quite thoroughly for some time.

"This is just so much to take in, you surely know how to rile up your guests with a swiftness Mr. Reid, hah."

"That I do. Now, I will ask you one final time. Will you join me so that we both will be able to achieve that which we most desire in the world? If you reject my offer, you are free to leave and ridicule me as you see fit when you go back to your home. But, if you accept...there will be no going back. No matter the cost or what we shall see, you must persevere and continue. So, what will it be?" Reid smiled and extended a hand out towards Doleman. Doleman looked at the artifact for a few moments before placing it in Reid's hand.

"I will work with you and perform the ritual alongside you. While I fear I will learn about things quite unsavory, I fear more that I will not. I look forward to working with you, Professor Reid."

***

"No, absolutely not. The very notion that I would even consider doing such a thing is beyond me and blasphemous to even think about. Mr. Reid, I strongly urge you to reconsider this plan of action before you put it into motion. Surely there are other methods available to us?" Doleman rummaged through the myriads of notes of the hickory table and flipped through dozens of pages of the Necronomicon. Reid let out an exasperated sigh.

"Unfortunately, we must cast aside any inkling of a moral code if we wish for the ritual to be a success. Mr. Doleman, all of our other preparations have been completed. These final two tasks are all that is left. We have no other choice but to become like the worshippers of Cybele. If we want to garner favor with the diabolic or angelic forces of the universe, then we must pay their prices." Doleman fell silent and threw the book down onto the table. He clenched the edges of the wood beneath his hands groaned from mental anguish.

"And you are quite certain that this...Gatekeeper will recompense us justly?" Reid's face hardened at the question.

"God's love to mettle in the affairs of men, do they not, Mr. Doleman?"

"I suppose they do, sir. But you are asking me to defile a corpse!" Doleman turned to his research partner, nostrils flaring. Reid, put a hand up to sate his anger.

"No, no, hang on a moment. All I ask is that you help me dig up her corpse, if anyone is going to acquire the necessary ingredients from skeletal remains, who better than her husband?"

"Perhaps that is true, but we are still digging up a body that has been put to rest. Have you no shame!" Doleman grabbed onto Reid's collar and shouted into his face.

"Unhand me! If it means I will be able to feel the soft embrace of my wife I would give up everything I have and I would do it again and again!" Reid screamed back. "You think I wish to see her remains? Eh? By all that is holy, I do not! It pains me, Mr. Doleman." Reid shoved the young researcher away. Doleman could not help but feel some sympathy for the elderly man. For him to go to such lengths and to react in such a way proved to him that it was with a pained heart he is pursuing such a dark path. However, something did not go unnoticed by Doleman.

"Fine, I will submit to this request of yours. Although, you mentioned that there were two final tasks that must be completed. If this is the first task, I tremble at the thought of what the second one would be. As long as it is not murder, I shall be content, regardless of the severity of the crime we must commit. Well, what is it?" Doleman ranted out as he poured himself a drink while denying the very thought that the stress was causing his ailments to start up again. Reid on the other hand looked away and off into empty space.

"Mr. Doleman, forgive this old man's barbarity." Doleman paused his hand, his lips scarcely touching the tip of his crystal glass filled with gin. Slowly and carefully, he placed the glass back down onto the table and pursed his lips.

"You would have us...become murderers."

"That is a bit too harsh given the circumstances."

"Come now Mr. Reid! Do not attempt to reduce the weight of the sins that we are going to commit. Be forthright and honest with me; are these the only two horrid tasks required of us?"

"In terms of depravity, yes. But, I can guarantee if we do them, we will be successful in attaining our respective goals. I know men such as ourselves should be dirtying our hands with such heinous nonsense, but we swore to each other that we would not go back. Not now."

The two men stared each other down, the gravity of what they were going to do gnawing at their minds. Finally, without averting his gaze, Doleman reached a hand out and Reid shook it in reply.

"The prize for the cost...I deem it to be worthy. I am by no means excited or elated at the atrocious acts I will commit in the pursuit of knowledge. But...from everything I have learned from this accursed text and from your journeys. I know that I am on the cusp of something amazing beyond all measure." A grim smile morphed its way onto Doleman's face, with Reid returning one in kind.

"The feeling is mutual. I am happy we were able to come to a consensus on these matters. It truly would have been a shame if we paused here, as I would not be able to do these things without you, Mr. Doleman." Reid said, going back to his litany of papers and notes. The two bid each other goodnight as they had spent hours deciphering the ritual from the Necronomicon as well as furthering their own knowledge.

Before leaving, however, they decided that they would enact the first task of theirs the following night around midnight. It was forecasted that the weather would be most cumbersome; down pouring rain and mist. Of course, this was noted to be very ominous by Doleman, but Reid found it to be fantastic. They would have the elements on their side to hide the sounds of their digging as well as their forms from all possible prying eyes. Doleman relented and dropped the matter and the two went to bed.

***

Two gentlemen cloaked in robes grey, shovels gripped in their hands entered through the rusted Eastern gate to the cemetery. At first glance, the men had believed they would be unable to enter due to a lock on the gate. But, upon further inspection learned that the lock was severely rusted and damaged thanks to the exposure from the elements for untold years.

After evading a rather portly and lazy looking watchmen, the two companions made their way to Reid's wife's tombstone.

He Lies Beatrice Reid, 1850-1915. Read the well-kept yet drenched tombstone. Doleman heard Reid mutter a slight prayer asking for forgiveness not from a higher power, but instead from his deceased wife.

The two then set to work as they were buffeted by rain and sleet that pricked their exposed faces. It would have been a humorous sight to see these two men uncoordinated and unhealthy men dig as they did. Reid had not the body of a man used to manual labor due to his age, and Doleman, being ill for most of his life, was thin and thought of to be very fragile by those who saw him. Odd how the intellectual works his mind yet neglects their bodies.

Finally, after several hours the exhausted pair cast aside their mud-encrusted shovels, panting heavily as they gazed down at the casket beneath their feet. Reid then picked up a lantern they had brought along and lit the candle within it. He then told Doleman to watch out for the pesky guard in case he actually does his job and gets the jump on the two men. Agreeing, Doleman looked around like a sentinel, investigating every agitated movement with his studious eyes.

Reid carefully eased himself down into the pit and set aside his lantern. He placed a hand on the face of the casket, his fingers caressing the golden cross with closed eyes. With a regretful hand, he then lifted open the casket and placed a wet hand over his mouth as tears welled up in his eyes.

There, feet away from his head laid the bones of his dearly departed wife. Even though she was now a skeleton and her once elegant red dress was frayed and stained from decay. Reid could still picture her there, his Beatrice, sleeping there unbothered by the rain spilling onto her.

"Forgive your husband my darling, he only wishes to love you once again." With those words spoken Reid scanned his wife's skeleton for loose fragments of bone if any that he could take with him as he shuddered at the thought of mutilating the remains. As luck would have it, if one would call it luck in this situation, saw a rather large hole in the skull and found a little pool of red within it.

Taking a vial and cap out from his cloak, he dipped it into the pool of blood and captured it. Once the vial was secure, Reid placed it back into his robe and then picked up the lantern.

"Mr. Doleman, I now require your assistance." Doleman wandered over to the hole and asked what he may need. "You must help take the casket with us."

"Pardon me? I was under the assumption that all we were going to gather were bone fragments or fluids if some should remain after all these years." An incredulous Doleman responded.

"For the ritual to work, we need to bring her with us so that she will be reanimated! Now make haste Doleman, we haven't much time. The longer we stay out, the faster we may be apprehended by an authority!"

"For Pete's sake!" Doleman worked his way down into the pit with Reid and hoisted the now closed casket up with great strain and settled it down onto the ground while they caught their breaths. A voice, slightly muddled by the downfall of rain caught them by surprise.

"Well, it appears you two blokes are in quite the conundrum, yeh?" The two researchers turned around slowly as they cursed under their breath.

"Sir, I beg of you to look the other way, I shall pay you handsomely if you do so," Reid said with confidence, positive that the lowly watchmen of a cemetery would quickly comply.

"I am afraid not. I have been working at these godforsaken place all of my life and finally, I have caught not one, but two grave robbers. Do you know what kind of money I would get if I turned you boys into Scotland Yard? Plenty!" The man laughed aloud, over the rain. Even from the few feet that separated them, Doleman could smell the liquor on the man's breath. He was also balding, missing several teeth, and had a meaty face that obscured his beady eyes.

"Please, sir, grant us this mercy. You see, this is the casket of the wife of my dear friend here. He merely wishes to take her to be buried elsewhere." Doleman lied through his teeth. The watchmen crossed his arms, appearing as though he considered the plea for a moment but shrugged after a brief moment.

"No, sorry lads. This is the end of your adventure. Now come with me and don't make this harder on yourselves." The man waved a hand at the pair to follow him, and when they refused to move, pulled out a club. "Don't make me use this boys. There is no reason for us to come to blows. You know I am only doing my job, and that is that. Now come along." Again, the two men refused to move. Doleman's eyes also looked downward at the shovel he had discarded earlier for the briefest of moments, a horrible idea flashing across his mind.

"Fine, fine, young man we will comply with your demand. Just put the club away, alright?" Happy with this, the oaf put away his weapon and Reid began to walk with his arms up to showcase his submission. And while Doleman was obscured behind him, quickly bent low and picked up the shovel. With one swift motion swung the back of the shovel against the man's forehead, knocking him out instantly.

"With that, we can satisfy both of the tasks to be completed." Doleman, feeling a bit ill, threw the shovel down again and emptied the contents of his gut onto the ground. "Sorry for that, it appears I have once again fallen prey to an illness I have long tangled with since my youth.

"No, that is fine Mr. Doleman. Once you recover your muscle we shall load the casket into my carriage and then tie up the watchmen and bring him along with us. He shall be used as the sacrifice for the ritual to summon That Which Lurks In The Dark." Nodding, and spitting the disgusting taste from his mouth, Doleman roused up some energy to complete what was asked.

The two men then carried the casket of Beatrice to the buggy and placed it in an attached cart. While there, Reid took some rope and brought it along with them back to the grave and paused in terror as the watchman's body was gone. Perplexed at the speed with which the man had recovered the two looked around wildly for him.

Unfortunately, being exhausted had caused them to be tackled down to the ground by the enraged sentinel.

"Knock me out will ya!" He roared, punching Doleman square in the face while Reid weakly got to his feet. To prevent his elder from being set up again, Doleman held on tightly to the man, arms around his neck, causing him to thrash about wildly on top of him. Their struggle persisted for little over ten more seconds before the familiar sound of metal hitting bone shot through the air. The watchman then collapsed, a pained groan escaping his lips.

Reid was seen standing above Doleman taking deep breaths.

"Now we must hurry, there is no telling when this brawny Neanderthal will awaken yet again," Reid said as he helped roll the large man off Doleman. "Now, help me bind our foe so that he may be of use to use yet."

"Are we not going to end his life here?" Doleman questioned.

"No, he shall be the catalyst by which we complete the ritual. That will come later. Please, no more questions, we have to transport our cargo before more try to stop or apprehend us." Doleman ceased his inquiries mostly due to having exerted much of his stamina and did as Reid instructed.

Terribly weary and completely drenched, the duo returned to the buggy and cart and quickly rode back to Reid's mansion.

Fortunately for the pair, they did not run into any lawmen on their ride back. For if they did, they most likely would have spent the remainder of their days spent in a cell, going mad not knowing what would have been.

Upon their return, they further tied the man up in an upstairs guest room that was windowless and locked the door behind them. As for the casket, it was haphazardly placed in the large living room, as the men were too tired to move it farther than that.

The two men then wordlessly went to bed to rest prior to the night that was to come the next day.

***

The watchman, who the two men learned was named Terrence after a profanity-laden rant detailing how he would murder the pair, was gagged prior to leaving Reid's mansion. While the ritualistic sacrifice would be occurring during the middle of the night on private property, the last thing Doleman and Reid wanted was to have to fend off more men powerful than them.

"Other than not keeping this man longer than we necessary for the ritual, why are we conducting it on this particular night, Mr. Reid?" Doleman asked as he helped carry the now unconscious Terrence to the clearing behind the mansion.

"The first day of August was marked as the prime day for the chances of success being the highest...now, drop the man here." He grunted. The pair not so gently dropped the portly watchman onto a circular stone slab with runes inscribed that resembled the ones on the protective artifact Reid had shown prior. The slab itself was of sandstone and was completely dry despite the minor rain and gusts of periodic wet wind. This slab in particular was around waist-high to the two men and could easily fit two prone bodies upon it, exactly what they wanted. How this was constructed, Doleman did not know but was certain Reid had commissioned its construction long before his arrival to the mansion.

Around the slab were four standing stones around ten feet in height and three feet in width. All of them were pasty white and once again had those odd runes inscribed on them. Doleman found this to be peculiar, as the Necronomicon did not state that this was necessary. However, he deduced that Reid simply wanted to make their ritual as safe as possible, seeing that they would be calling upon forces that mere mortals could not comprehend. Still, he was concerned and asked Reid if this would have any negative effect on themselves or the ritual itself.

"Nonsense! How could something that stands for protection lead to one's own destruction? Get those jitters out of you Mr. Doleman; I have done so long ago. Come, we still have much to do before the appointed time." Reid grunted, rather annoyed.

"Very well. Help me tie the man down then." Doleman and Reid then proceeded to fit four metal spikes into the open slots on the slab. Both of them hammered away at them until they were around halfway in and once they were sure metal stakes were secure, tied a rope around them. The end of each rope was then tied to around the wrists and ankles of the watchmen. The reasons for this were obvious; to keep his body steady when they ended his life and to make certain he would not escape like the previous night.

The two men walked sorely back to the rear entrance of the mansion and picked up the casket with great difficulty thanks to muscular discomfort. Then, with great effort on the part of them both, carried it to the stone slab like two devilish pallbearers. Once they reached the slab they dropped it not as elegantly as they had hoped and the casket dropped down with some force, eliciting a cracking sound that pierced through the slow downfall of rain and wind.

Reid let out an exasperated sigh and apologized to his wife for the rough way they had treated her skeletal remains. Doleman, empathizing with the man, apologized as well, but more for what they were about to do. All that was needed for them to do was bring out the text of Alhazred and finally have their hard work pay off.

It was ultimately decided by the pair that it would be Reid himself who would conduct the entirety of the ritual for two reasons. The first being that while he was much older than Doleman, he had a much firmer resolve and not as squeamish as his younger companion. The second reason was that Doleman had become frightfully ill over the course of the past several days. The stress of the recent events and the constant moral battle within him combined with his weak immunity to illness made him rather infirm at the moment. And the last thing they needed was for something to worry about when they got down to business.

However, wanting to be of a little more use, Doleman went inside himself in order to retrieve the text and bring it back as quickly as he could. But, when he laid his hands on the book of the dead, he hesitated. He then looked at his reflection in a nearby mirror and recoiled at the face looking back at him. His face looked to be devoid of life with its sickly pale color and his once-vibrant green-colored eyes were now dulled. Turning his head from side to side he could that his cheekbones were protruding out very noticeably.

Closing his eyes and bowing his head, he wanted nothing more than to leave after seeing what had become of him. But, he knew he could not. In spite of his moral qualms, his earthly desires proved too great to overcome and so firmly grasped the book and brought it to the waiting Reid.

"Wonderful, now, let us begin and acquire what we deserve." Reid grinned widely and opened to the required page for the invocation he needed and spoke the words he had wanted to say for years. "Y'AI'NG'NGAH, YOG-SOTHOTH, H'EE-L'GEB, F'AI THRODOG, UAAAH!" Immediately on hearing those words worm their way into his ears, Doleman shrieked and covered them. "Fear not Mr. Doleman! We are safe. Us not being dead on the ground is proof of that!" Doleman ignored this and instead focused on not losing control of his mental faculties, how Reid had such mental resistance however, he did not know.

Reid then pulled out an ornate and brilliantly shining silver dagger from his coat and raised it high above his head, aiming at the poor watchman's heart. And with a single stab, pierced the man's chest as he hollered into the waking world before falling silent as death carried him off. Not needing the knife anymore, he left it sticking out of the limp body and then chanted once again those foul words he used to initiate the invocation after taking the vial of blood from his pocket and sprinkling it over his wife's casket.

He chanted louder and louder as he set the book down on the stone and extended his arms out, ready to receive the coming of Yog.

Doleman was now on his knees, all of his senses panicking wildly as the ground began to shake beneath him and the area around them grew dark, as though cutting them off from the rest of the world. A terrible stench then filled his nostrils and a purplish mist settled down all and caused his eyes to water. But, what surprised Doleman the most was that regardless of his increasing fear, the scent was disturbingly intoxicating.

Reid chanted the invocation one final time with as much force as his body could muster and upon finishing it, an enormous rift in the sky appeared. From that diabolical wound, an entity of grandiose madness gilded its way through, staining the world with its blasphemous presence. The two men gawked, eyes wide with mouths agape at what they beheld.

Therefrom the void and incomprehensible and colossal behemoth of infinite knowledge and power and corruption entered thusly into the world.

It vaguely resembled the painting Reid had shown Doleman but only now did the two feel its awesome power. It appeared to be mostly enormous and bulbous colorful orbs that change colors rapidly. Surrounding such orbs were tangles of brown and fleshy, squirming tentacles. Beneath such fluid moving tendrils were millions of mouths gnawing at the very fabric of existence while others screamed terrible things that both Doleman and Reid did not wish to believe.

Thankfully, the little artifact and the runic inscriptions did as Reid had promised as they glowed gold and offered some sort of resistance against the great deity before them. However, as it grew closer they could feel their bodies growing more and more corrupted as the seconds ticked on by. Therefore, they would have to act quickly before they were consumed.

"O, Yog-Sothoth! Grant me your aid, I ask of you to resurrect my lovely wife! I have given you a sacrifice worthy of one such as yourself, so make my desire reality!" Reid bowed his head, the veins under his skin now a dark and disgusting black. The monstrous profane being above them roared and then the casket on the slab rose slightly into the air and opened up.

The skeleton Beatrice rose up into the air and both men watched dumbfounded at how sinew, veins, blood, skin, organs wrapped themselves around the bones until Beatrice appeared in her prime.

"My Beatrice...it is truly you!" Reid cried out happily, tears of blackness falling down his cheeks. Doleman admitted that the woman was incredibly beautiful despite the method used to resurrect her. She had golden blonde hair, firm, and smooth looking skin. But, when she opened her pale-blue eyes and smiled, Doleman felt incredibly apprehensive. Reid failed to notice anything wrong thanks to his joy and told Doleman to quickly ask for his desires to be granted as well.

Struggling to his feet, Doleman shouted his request.

"Show me all that was, is, and will be! Let me bear witness to all that is hidden from mankind!" Again the beast roared from its millions of mouths, yet Doleman felt no change in his mind or body. Confused, he turned to Reid who was reaching a hand out towards his wife, but instead of a loving embrace, what followed shook Doleman to the core.

Hundreds of tentacles not dissimilar from the ones belonging to the beast in the sky had shot out from her body and wrapped themselves around Reid. Doleman shrank back in fear as Reid called out to him to save him before having the tendrils shove themselves down his throat, silencing him. Beatrice's body then melted itself down into a gross mass of flesh and wrapped around Reid, combining the two bodies into a disgusting abominable pile. Gutteral sounds escaped from the two mouths that opened up from below the flesh.

Taking another horrified step back, Doleman covered his mouth as long spikes extended out from the sinewy mound with strings of flesh connecting the two appendages creating some sort of a human harp or other string instruments.

"We allowed it to enter...past the protection," Doleman

whispered, realizing how the two had erred in the ritual, and only then did he also realize he had stepped out from the safety of the protective runes as well.

Doleman attempted to run as he heard the Beatrice/Reid gelatinous mound play their distorted melody from their flesh harp but fell to the ground as he felt his mind pierced by a force that transcended reality itself.

The world around him evaporated, as did his body, and found himself to now be a third-party observer. What he saw next was nothing short of blasphemous atrocity incarnate.

A gargantuan mass of horrors that squirmed and wiggled about. Gigantic tentacles and tendrils sprouted out from the center mass. Gaping maws littered the massive body as well as at the end of the tendrils. Orbs of flesh and claw-like appendages too were darted across the galaxy-sized horror. At the center of this affront to all creation was an enormous mouth filled with teeth the size of solar systems and behind them a void that held the secret to all that was and will be.

Surrounding the entity were misshapen geometric horrors with wildly flailing appendages that rapidly played instruments of unknown design in a cacophonous symphony, as though worshipping the monster they surrounded. But, at this point, Doleman knew what their purpose was.

These images faded away and now he beheld the answers to his questions. From outside the Earth's solar system, he saw a beast with the head of an octopod, with draconic wings and humanoid body travel to Earth, accompanied by miniature creatures that resembled this creature. They thusly settled on Earth and did battle with primal beings of chaos who resembled barrel-like creatures with odd wings, eye-stalks, and as an assortment of sinewy and stringlike growths. He then saw as the great beast from the stars settled under the waves of the oceans of Earth, falling into a deep sleep.

Next, he saw in a rapid fashion a lot of entities with forms most unnatural and human-like as they did what they pleased with Earth and the greater universe. Here did Doleman witness their interactions with humanity, as well as the secrets of humanity's inception. With fright did he learn of the true intended purpose of humanity, which he vehemently wished to deny, but knowing that his rejection of it would merit nothing. As the ages flew past his gaze, the cults of humans who worshipped these deities and the other alien life that littered the Earth in secret.

"Enough!" Doleman screamed, returning back to his corporeal form. He then fell silent for a moment and looked up at the now blank sky, void of the entity who had come. The gross fusion of his friend and his wife was now absent as well.

Doleman then began to laugh, starting out with a chuckle that turned into a violent fit of convulsive cheers and lamentations. Unable to cope with the answers that he received, he took both of his hands and shoved them deep into his eyes. Yanking them out, he threw them in a random direction, not even registering the pain.

"Blindness and death are preferable than to continue to be subject to the whims of those who care naught for their children!" He screamed in a moment of clarity before the wild madness from the knowledge that had been imparted to him consumed him. It was there on the muddy ground did he Robert Doleman breathe his last breath and expire from shock and blood loss.

The events of what occurred that night are not known by the authorities who investigated after reports of ground shakes in the area. Based on the bodies found and the ritualist altar, the incident was chalked up to be the work of a mad cult. Robert

Doleman was considered to not be a perpetrator of the unfortunate incident but instead was counted among the victims of it alongside the watchman he helped kidnapped. Jacob Reid however was classified as missing and was never found.

As for the book that brought about the ruin of the two men, it was 'lost' after it was brought in as evidence by local authorities and its location has not yet been discovered.

The truth of reality is a burden far too much to bear by any single man or even by collective humanity, for we lack the mental fortitude to resist the destruction wrought from such truth onto our psyche's.

THE EXPERIMENT

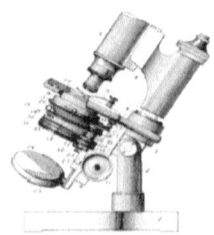

I was called in at 0200 hours, an unusual time for an autopsy. But so goes the life of a military medical examiner. With the Neo Cold War in full swing, 1995 was proving a deadly year for both sides.

They told me that they had a field operative who had been the victim of some unknown chemical or biological weapon of the opposition forces. They want me to figure out what killed the poor bastard. It shouldn't be that hard for me hell, I've created enough biological agents over the years to stockpile both sides in this conflict. This one shouldn't be that hard to decipher.

With a fresh pot of coffee and the whole night before me, I dove into my work with unfettered enthusiasm. Finally I was able to peer into what the other side was using against us in this secret and clandestine conflict.

The cadaver lying before me was retrieved from his

residence two days ago and was already deceased and in a partially mutated state. When I uncovered the body I was shocked to see a deformed and mutated human form that barely looked like an anthropoid homo sapien. I

His, or should I say "its" head was large and malformed, the size and shape of a watermelon. The torso was a mass or bulbous lesions and puss leaking polyps. The appendages were twisted and elongated to appear more like tentacles than arms and legs.

My mask and goggles would protect me from any exposure, but I didn't want too much distance from my subject, as a good forensic always needs to make a connection with his subordinate.

I started with a simple test to rule out biological exposure. The Only pathogen that causes cell deterioration this rapidly is Veselin Bovine Disease, but the symptoms were all wrong. The cell destruction was massive and there were lesions and malformed growths all over the carcass.

I thought it might have been Donoranian Granulomatis, but this would not account for the purplish color that his skin had taken on.

I decided to test for a neuro-pathogen. Back in the 1950s, when everyone was designing nerve gas for the Korean War, I was experimenting with genetic mutation. It was going to be a weapon, of course, and we made progress but in the end the project was abandoned. Some of the P>O.W.s that had "volunteered" as test subjects resembled the cadaver I had on the table.

I did a molecular fungus scan. Any detection of multicellular sporozoans or genetically engineered bacterium will give me some lead, some path to follow in my quest for the truth. This too yielded no results. I was getting frustrated, but loved the challenge. This was proving harder than expected.

Whoever the biologist was who created this bio-weapon was a more formidable foe than I had previously thought.

My superiors thought it would be best to record the autopsy. It would be used as a teaching tool for future postmortem dissections. The computer link-up was the idea of a new breed of pathologists. Even though I don't trust new technologies, I must admit it was helping me in my findings. But enough with the dermal examination, it was time to dig right in.

My new micro-scalpel worked well with other victims, but this seemed to be a bit difficult. Even the razor sharp blade was not easily penetrating the leathery hide of which I had to keep reminding myself was human.

With a sharper blade and a more powerful implement I was able to cut my way through to the innards. The internal organs were equally ulcerated and lesioned. Whoever created this pathogen was a genius...a true artist in the alternative warfare field. I was jealous, how could anyone create such a perfect weapon. In all the years I spent with the C.I.A. I had created numerous biological agents for deployment in the war, but none like this.

The deformed organs that spilled out of the body cavity were covered in a noxious yellow goop. My forceps were of no use to me, besides, no tools were better than my own hands. With my sterile latex gloves I proceeded to reach inside and see what was lurking about. My fingers discovered all sorts of misshapen entrails and tissue. Nothing resembled anything human, and I wondered for a minute if I had before me some alien-human hybrid that the alien conspiracy nuts had always been harping about.

The brains were liquefied, the bones dissolved, the organs fused. Strewn before me on the table was a magnificent display of gnarled and grotesque viscera, the likes of which I'd never seen. Now that I had extracted the internal carnage the real fun could begin.

With all of these new specimens, I was sure to reach a conclusion. Under the microscope, the gram-stained samples still revealed nothing. Not even *coiled filament bacillus*.

After twelve hours I was spent, but eager to continue. My sixth cup of coffee was doing no good, and may have been giving my hand the jitters.

The more I studied this subject, the more I wanted to shake the hand of its creator. I surmised the pathogen had concentrated itself in the organs. I checked for gelatinous infiltration of the spleen, commonly associated with *Anthrax Bacillus*. I thought this microorganism could be a derivative. With Anthrax, death was common in twenty four to forty eight hours, and this could be the cause, but it doesn't explain the massive tissue degeneration.

The Anthrax culture as negative.

I decided to examine the scabbed lesions on the subject's liver. Upon treating them with *atrophene sulphate*, I noticed no suppression of chemotoxicity. I therefore ruled out the presence of an *organophosphate neurotoxin*.

A spinal tap revealed a lessening of the internal fluids, but this still brought me no closer to a conclusion.

My examination of the other internal organs was a more burdensome task than I had foreseen. I had trouble distinguishing the gall bladder from the kidneys. This soldier's insides were a gnarled quagmire of flesh and bone. The vision before me would have inspired the best of the abstract expressionists. And this...this excited me. Whoever designed this microbe was not only brilliant, but also a composer of perfection. Was this his first attempt? Or his pièce de résistance?

I needed to delve deeper into this mystery. Time was running out and I was not going to be made a fool of, my superiors were watching. I had to prove I was the more astute scientist than my unknown adversary. I had to decipher this horrid yet beautiful plague, but I was at a standstill, I had tried everything.

On impulse, I grabbed my drill. I decided to do some random drilling. I thought it might reveal something. The spinning saw-blade cut into the thick cadaver with ease and the internal fluids shot everywhere. I didn't care that my protective gear were now covered in potentially hazardous contaminants, I thought that for sure this would reveal something...something I hadn't seen before.

The sound of the drill piercing the cadaver was like music to my ears, never had it sounded so melodic.

And my toys. I looked around at the joyful assortment of scalpels, retractors and laparoscopic instruments and I was emphatic. I had so many toys to choose from. I just wanted to use them all. My pliers, they never looked so shiny and pointy. They were so good for picking and digging. I couldn't understand why I had become so giddy about my surgeon's tools.

Maybe it was because I was on the verge of discovering a brand new biological weapon. My hands were trembling uncontrollably. I let my pliers lead the way; they were compelling me to dig my way to the gastrointestinal tract. *My God*, I thought, was this where the virus resides?

I dug deep and peered inside the dark mucous covered cavity of my wondrous specimen. I couldn't believe it, but the innards were pulsing. It could not be. I blinked and tried to wipe my sludge covered goggles, but it was true. Somehow, the deceased tissue was coming to life. The intestines began to move. I watched as the once departed forms squirmed to life like incongruous worms. I stepped back, but the writhing mass was reaching for me like some nightmarish squid.

Like some disproportioned roundworms, the creature's tentacles emerged from the body cavity and lunged at me.

GOOD GOD, I thought, what type of weapon is this? One that lays dormant, and for all intent and purposes can be pronounced dead at the cellular level, only to rise once again at a predetermined time? Had I unlocked this monstrosity? Was it being controlled by an outside force?

I barely had time to deduce all the possibilities, when the slime-covered appendages wrapped themselves around my neck and torso. Like a boa constrictor crushing its next meal, I felt the life squeezing out of me. Before I took my final breath, I heard the door to the autopsy room open.

I tried to speak, I tried to warn them not to come in, the bio-contagion was alive, it was infectious, tried as I might, I could not make the words. As the life was drained out of me, I could see three shadowy figures standing before me. They spoke.

"Delusions, hallucinations, paranoia," the man dressed in a five-star general's garb said with a smirk, "Congratulations, doctor, the experiment was a success."

Success? Was he insane? Could he not see me strangled on the floor, near death, a victim of a reanimated biological contamination?

"The experimental Dionyceogen we slipped into your

coffee caused insanity in less than two hours," the man in the physician's attire said, "just as we predicted.

What? Was I the victim of a bio-weapon by my own government?

"Notify the president that his political challenger will be having his mental breakdown right on schedule," the military brass man explained, "right in the middle of the televised debates."

Had I not been attacked by a tentacled procreation? I tried desperately to grasp what sanity I had left. I blinked and tried to focus my eyes; to my disbelief there was nothing around my neck except my own hands. I looked up at my examination table, and saw nothing more than a normal human carcass!

As I felt the last semblance of my sanity leave my poor battered brain, I heard the final words that sent a chill up my spine.

"Prepare this quack for an autopsy," the authority figure laughed as he left the room and two orderlies came in and dragged me away.

"I want to know just how well this new weapon works."

ABOUT THE AUTHOR

Frank Forte is an accomplished writer, designer, storyboard artist and comic book artist. Frank's film and TV credits include: Lovecraft Country, Fantasy Island, Solar Opposites, Dreamwork's 3Below, Bob's Burgers, Insidious 4, Lego: Guardians of the Galaxy, Despicable Me 2, Lego Star Wars: The Empire Strikes Out, The Super Hero Squad Show, Marvel Heroes 4D, and Lego Hero Factory. Frank's comic book credits include: Heavy Metal Magazine, Bob's Burgers, Warlash, DTOX, Zombie Terrors and Chicken Soup For Satan among others.

Frank also writes books and novels. His two anthologies Beyond Lovecraft and Beyond Doomsday can be purchased on Amazon.com and through bookstores nationwide.

In Frank's spare time he paints. Influenced by classic cartoons and comic books, Frank's paintings are an assemblage of inspiration from what he grew up watching on TV and reading in comic books. Trying to capture the feeling and emotion of a moving cartoon on a flat canvas, Frank's work incorporates horrific and twisted subjects in disturbingly bizarre situations. His work has been exhibited at the La Luz De Jesus Gallery, Copro Gallery, Corey Helford Gallery, CASS Contemporary, Dark Art Emporium, Arch Enemy Arts, Phone Booth Gallery, Night Gallery

Fine Arts, Cannibal Flower, LTD. Gallery and Hyaena Gallery.

Frank is also the publisher at Asylum Press (http://www.asylumpress.com), an indy graphic novel and comic book publisher. Asylum Press is a publishing company that produces premium comic books and graphic novels within the horror, science fiction, and action genres.

Frank Forte links

www.FrankForte.com

www.facebook.com/FrankForteArt

www.twitter.com/FrankForteart

www.instagram.com/FrankForteArt/

ABOUT THE PUBLISHER

Asylum Press is a publishing company that produces premium books, comic books and graphic novels within the horror, science fiction, fantasy, thriller and action genres. We then maximize the value of these branded properties by extending them across multiple media platforms, including movies, TV, and video games, often using transmedia storytelling techniques and social networking to reach a much broader audience than traditional comic book publishers do.

Our books feature original, character-driven stories and cinematic artwork by top creators and newly discovered talent that will appeal to not only comic book fans, but also mainstream fiction readers who don't normally buy comics.

Over the last year, we've worked hard to recruit the best artists we can find from around the world and team them up with professional screenwriters to create exceptional material that will captivate readers. We believe quality still matters in this industry.

Asylum Press delivers high-concept books via a business model that focuses on digital publishing and new distribution outlets in both the American and international markets.

Asylum Press links

www.asylumpress.com

www.facebook.com/AsylumPress

www.twitter.com/asylumpress

www.instagram.com/asylumpress

www.youtube.com/user/AsylumPress

ABOUT GOON CARTOONS

Goon Cartoons is a creator and curator of funny cartoons, animation, and short films. Featuring: *the Ultra Mega Super Squad, Cut It Out, Buck Billy, The Cletus and Floyd Show, Billy Boy, The Struggle* and more. Goon Cartoons is a proud member of Channel Frederator.

SUBSCRIBE for updates, we upload a new cartoons three times per week.

http://www.youtube.com/user/GoonCartoons?sub_confirmation=1

Goon Cartoons YouTube channel can be found here:

https://www.youtube.com/user/GoonCartoons

Instagram

https://www.instagram.com/gooncartoons/

Facebook

https://www.facebook.com/GoonCartoons/

Twitter

https://twitter.com/gooncartoons

Goon Cartoons official website:

www.gooncartoons.com

About Michael du Plessis

Michael du Plessis teaches Comparative Literature at the University of Southern California. She is the author of a novel, *The Memoirs of JonBenet by Kathy Acker*, and has written and published poetry and essays on topics that range from queer 'zines to Goth music to British science fiction of the 1960s.